I0595790

Samuel Longfellow, Joseph May

Memoir and Letters

Samuel Longfellow, Joseph May

Memoir and Letters

ISBN/EAN: 9783744687379

Printed in Europe, USA, Canada, Australia, Japan

Cover: Foto ©Raphael Reischuk / pixelio.de

More available books at **www.hansebooks.com**

SAMUEL LONGFELLOW

MEMOIR AND LETTERS

EDITED BY

JOSEPH MAY

MINISTER OF THE FIRST UNITARIAN CHURCH OF PHILADELPHIA

" Speak, Lord, for thy servant heareth "

BOSTON AND NEW YORK
HOUGHTON, MIFFLIN AND COMPANY
The Riverside Press, Cambridge
1894

Copyright, 1894,
By HOUGHTON, MIFFLIN & CO.

All rights reserved.

The Riverside Press, Cambridge, Mass.. U.S.A.
Electrotyped and Printed by H. O. Houghton and Company.

PREFACE

HENRY WADSWORTH LONGFELLOW was once greatly pleased when a friend referred to him as "the brother of a poet." He fully appreciated the implication.

The poet intended was Samuel Longfellow, whose memory it is sought to perpetuate by the publication of this volume.

Not deficient, as his beautiful hymns attest, in that power of poetical expression with which genius so richly endowed the elder Longfellow, Samuel shared fully with his gifted brother the poetic instinct and the poet's temperament.

In dignity and simplicity of character; in sweetness and serenity of disposition; in the single love of truth, and in the pure spirituality of his life and all its motives, no man ever surpassed him. The desire to present an example of such traits is the justification of this sketch, and of the extracts from Mr. Longfellow's corre-

spondence, which are the most significant part
of it.

"Letters," he writes, "do not read as well in
print as in manuscript." It may be that his own
will here have lost something of their charm,
and will not manifest all, or even much, of what
he was, except to those who knew him in life.
Yet it is hoped that enough of his spirit may
linger in them to reveal his character in fair
degree to such as first meet him in these pages.

A just account of Samuel Longfellow must
have adequately disclosed his interior life, in
which lay the reality of the man and of his
career. The only person who could have written
such an account of him was his friend, Samuel
Johnson, — but for him Mr. Longfellow had per-
formed this loving service. It has been left for
an inferior hand, and one not qualified by intimate acquaintance, to gather up these scanty
relics of a saintly history, and cast them into
such shape as it might.   J. M.

Philadelphia, April 15, 1894.

CONTENTS

SAMUEL LONGFELLOW

I

CHILDHOOD AND YOUTH

SAMUEL LONGFELLOW was born on the eighteenth day of June, 1819, in the beautiful city of Portland, Maine. That city has always had a peculiar charm for the hearts of its people, and in beginning his memoir of his brother, Mr. Longfellow dwells with affectionate admiration on its broad streets, arched with tall trees; its flanking hills; its spacious, island-dotted harbor, where the mightiest ships may ride; and the varied landscape westward, stretching over valleys and hills and forests, till it terminates in the shadowy vision of Mount Washington.

Hither all his life he loved to return; here, when the end was nigh, he found himself; and here, where it began, his earthly career terminated, — a career than which none was ever gentler, kinder, truer to conviction, or more firm in rectitude.

His birthplace was a house, now venerable with over a century of age, and standing among great elms in the midst of the bustle of the city. Seventy years ago it was on the outskirts of the town, almost a rural abode. It was noted as being the first brick dwelling built in Portland. Mr. Longfellow's maternal grandfather, General Peleg Wadsworth, had erected it ; and his father, Stephen Longfellow, had added to it a third story as his family grew.

There were eight children in the household, four sons, four daughters ; and Samuel was the youngest. Of their family life he gives, in the memoir of his brother, a charming picture, which no one else may venture to reproduce. It was refined, orderly, and religious ; but easy and cheerful. Parents were respected, but loved still more, and not feared. Brothers and sisters lived together in a perfect mutual affection which the passage of many years could not weaken. The father, a classmate at Harvard College of Judge Story and Dr. Channing, and the intimate friend of the latter, stood high in the community as a citizen and member of the bar. In 1814 he represented his district in the Legislature of Massachusetts, and eight years later, Maine having become a State, he sat for a term in the lower House of the National Congress. Politically he was a Federalist ; in religion, he had followed the liberalizing tendencies of the time, which, from a moderate Calvinism, were shaping the older Unitarianism. If the tradition repeated by his son is correct, that it was at his instance that the covenant of the First Parish of Portland was modified in the direction of progressive thought, we may have a hint of the source of the son's ever-forward look, and his strictness of fidelity to personal convictions, however finely distinguished.

For his mother, Samuel Longfellow throughout his life cherished a peculiar, tender devotion. She was a lineal descendant of John Alden and Priscilla Mullens. Of slight figure and expressive countenance, as he describes her, she retained through many later years of invalidism the traces of early beauty. From her he may well have inherited his exceeding sensitiveness ; his love of beauty in nature and in all the forms of art ; his serene and cheerful disposition ; his fortitude in suffering ; and especially his clear, intuitive, spiritual faith and childlike piety. " She was," he says, " a kind friend and neighbor ; a helper of the poor ; a devoted mother to her children, whose confidant she was ; the sharer of their little secrets and their joys ; the ready comforter of their troubles ; the patient corrector of their faults."

Thus, in an atmosphere of affection and comfort, of culture and religion, the boy's life began. There are signs that he was not only the youngest, but also the darling of the family. His traits may well have fitted him to be such. Of somewhat delicate organization, yet healthy and hearty, fond of fun, and peculiarly susceptible to the ludicrous, he was, as an early friend describes him, intelligent without precocity ; by no means wanting in masculine qualities ; and not unsocial, though fond of his own companionship, and rather the intimate friend of a select few than the hail-fellow of the many.

In one of his youthful poems he describes himself as " a dreamy child." He was quiet, but happy ; full of fancies of his own ; early coming to love reading, writing, and sketching ; preferring these, and in summer botanizing and the cultivation of his garden, and long rambles in the woods and fields, to the more usual sports of boys. Besides their own ample home, with its books, music, and evening games, the family was blest with a grandfather's home at Gorham, a few miles away, and, in earlier days, another, somewhat farther, where the children always had a welcome from their venerable relatives, and could enjoy a taste of country life and the habits of the farm. In the youthful poem we have referred to, Samuel calls up the happy hours spent in these scenes, and it may be that he had them in mind when, late in life, he said : "I always love to look upon a picture of a pine-tree ; it reminds me of my boyhood."

School life opened under the guiding care of two female teachers, and at the proper age, passing from their charge, he was entered at the well-known "Portland Academy" to prepare for college life. Master Bezaleel Cushman was now reigning, and Samuel seems to have been on terms of friendship with his preceptor, to judge from one kindly epistle of the latter to his pupil, which still exists in the accurate and florid manuscript of the old-time pedagogue.

The curriculum was the usual classical course of the day, with French, which was apparently well taught. At fourteen, a boyish journal shows Samuel reviewing the second book of the Georgics, and beginning the fourth of the Æneid ; reading Græca Minora ; and writing as well as reading French, which he likes, and with which he freely ornaments his diary. He appears to have been diligent, but not to the exclusion of occasional lapses. One Thursday, "got to school late, and missed my French lesson ; no matter (that is, *not much*)," — conscience speaking in the parenthesis. Perhaps this tardiness was due to his brother Henry's being "at home, for a day, from college."   But quite as likely because of another visitor, of the kind that always charmed him, a baby boy : " he is a little dear, and something prettier than he 'used to was,' formerly." Next day, alas, another deficiency, perhaps from the same causes : "had not time to get my lesson in Virgil."   On Saturday he rejoices, too, in the accidental exemption from a duty which may well have been distasteful to him.   "We did not declaim, to my great joy, for I had no piece but 'Pizarro,' and that is *so* old."

Religious culture was conducted according to the orderly customs of the time.   The two services of Sunday were a matter of course.   But there is a trace of positive interest in them, in Samuel's record of the texts and intelligent comments on the sermons.   One or two may have made a lasting impression.   The minister of the First Parish was Rev. Dr. Nichols, revered and beloved by his people through many years, and some of whose writings were as household words among the Unitarians of the period generally. One afternoon he "preached from Luke, 'Wist ye not that I must be about my Father's business?'   The sermon was upon what he termed the moral energy of Christ, which he said appeared to him a more striking feature in his

character than his gentleness and benevolence."
On January 27, "Mr. Whitman, from Saco,
preached, and, as usual, gave us a very good sermon. Text, 'I can do all things, through Christ
who strengtheneth me.' It was incumbent on
Christians, he said, to bear the misfortunes and
trials of life in a peculiar and Christlike manner ;
and to do this, they needed a strength greater
than their own ; this strength was to be derived
from their religion and from observing and imi-
tating the example of Christ. . . . In the afternoon we had another good sermon, upon Christian moderation, from Philippians iv." . . . On
February 10, in the evening, "went to St. Paul's
to hear the new minister. I have heard him
once before, on Christmas Day. Do not like him
much. He has a very careless manner of reading the prayers and exercises, sometimes fast
and sometimes slow."

Sunday-school had now been established, but
it made, perhaps, little impression on the boy's
mind, and received no record, except on a single
occasion.

One Saturday : "It was the turn of our class
to go to Dr. Nichols's this afternoon, and Edward
Weed called for me. Dr. N. told us that his
purpose in having the classes at his house was
not so much to hear their lessons, though that

was one reason ; but that he might become acquainted with the children. He thought a great deal of early impressions, he said. After he had heard us recite he showed us a microscope and gave us a shock with an electrical machine."

Samuel Longfellow, as a man, in his own pastorates, knew well how to copy and to improve on this genial and natural method of reaching young minds and hearts.

Besides school and church and Sunday-school, the boy was seasonably introduced to good literature. The world was still in the fresh delight of Scott's poems and novels, and Edgeworth lay on every well-ordered table, especially where there were children. Samuel began to find his way among these and other standard authors, and confided his artless criticisms to his diary. He much preferred "The Betrothed" to "The Talisman." Of "Castle Rackrent," he decided : "I do not like it much, though perhaps it is a good delineation of Irish character." "Charlotte Temple" he thought only "so-so-ish."

He sought also other opportunities of intellectual culture ; attending, by himself or with a school-friend, courses of lectures on natural science, on which he variously comments as "interesting" or "tedious." Occasionally, on a Saturday, he would drop into court to hear some noted pleader. The artifices of the rhetoricians did not escape his observation. Of one, "he is a good speaker, but rather 'agonizing' sometimes; for instance, 'did you not mark, gentlemen, the downcast eye and quivering lip, etc.'" With a crony, he penetrated an artist's studio. The painting "which most struck my fancy was a view of Sebago." Two portraits, by another artist, were "very pretty, but extra-like the originals." One evening, with the same companion, he "attended a concert by the band. It was very 'fine,' I believe, but not at all to *my* taste. The music is quite too loud and noisy for me." In these sincerities and refinements the boy was father of the man.

Amid such simple, happy experiences and surroundings, the period of boyhood was passing away. An occasional journey to the White Hills; picnics on the islands of the harbor; rambles in Deering's Woods; haying and egg-gathering at a grandfather's farm, made the summers pleasant in fact and as lifelong memories. Winter tasks and the instructions of Master Cushman were preparing the youth for college and life.

II

COLLEGE

MAKING his way alone, by steamer, to Boston, Samuel Longfellow entered Harvard College as a Freshman in the summer of 1835. He was sixteen years old, and brought to college the reputation of a fine scholar; a love for good literature and for the beautiful in all its forms; an inquiring mind; a sensitive conscience; a strong will for the right; and a heart which was to open, erelong, with singular responsiveness, to religious impressions and the suggestions of spiritual things.

There remains little record of the incidents of his college life. "I can only recollect," writes his chum of the first year, Rev. Dr. Nichols, son of his pastor and an old school-fellow, "that my regard and affection for him were daily increased by this closest contact which one young man has with another." While he inclined, as in boyhood, to intimate relations with a few friends rather than to general acquaintanceship, he was well-known, never recluse or unsocial, and took a hearty interest in all college affairs. He was an active

member of the leading societies, including the
Institute, the A. Δ. Φ., the Hasty Pudding Club,
of which he was secretary, and the Φ. B. K., and
his gift as a versifier was often employed to
provide the songs called for at their meetings
and on the various occasions of college festivity,
or a poem at some anniversary celebration.

A few stray letters reflect amusingly the events
and issues of these happy days: —

"A. Δ. Φ. flourishes like any green *baize* tree,
as Sam says. The essays are regular, and the
secretary scolds the brother-scribes in the warmest spirit allowed by the constitution. Another
effort is to be made to secure recognition by the
Faculty. The Geneva Chapter, for a similar end,
were obliged to elect in one of the Faculty, and
chose the President, who was to be initiated
with great pomp. Imagine him swearing eternal friendship with Sophomores, and wearing a
breastpin!"

"Do you ever meet any traveling brethren of
the Fraternity? I confess, for my part, I rather
favor the plan of the Brunonians for dissolving the
whole concern, as opposed to the 'spirit of the
age.' The idea of invisible bonds, and secret
leagues, and swearing eternal friendship to hun-
dreds of people one has never seen, is better
suited to chivalric times than to these days of

ours when everybody chooses to go on his own hook."

Longfellow's habits of study, in college, though not highly methodical, were diligent and attentive, and gave him both good standing in his class and the repute of ability and promise. His bent was especially for the classics, for English literature, and for history. "He was," says a classmate, "easily our best writer." "What he did not know about belles-lettres," writes another, "seemed to us not worth knowing." He continued the French of his school-days and added German, of which he became very fond, making sufficient progress in it to enable him, when a resident-graduate, to supply the place of the German instructor during an illness. It may be that his familiar acquaintance with Italian dates from college days. Natural science also interested him. Botany he had always loved, and he was now attracted to astronomy, for the study of which, with seven of his friends, he formed a club, called "The Octagon." The element of pleasure was not left out of this youthful organization, but they essayed something of serious work; going to the observatory to study the phenomena of the heavens, or watching the Northern Lights and meteors from their windows or convenient roofs. Papers were prepared and read at their meetings, and the memory of these hours pleasantly survived, as such recollections will, through all the later days of the little group. Writing from Portland, during a vacation, to his classmate and lifelong friend, Edward Everett Hale, he is anxious to know whether a remarkable aurora, of which he had slept unconscious on the steamer, had been observed by The Octagon; and discusses gravely, with a mind open to conviction, the existence of that perennial curiosity, the sea-serpent. The supposition that such a reptile might have survived from primeval times he thinks reasonable. That on their innumerable trips back and forth the officers of the coastwise steamers should never have seen one is a negative argument of weight.

Thus passed, as is evident from his subsequent letters and his enduring love for his college, four happy and useful years. The annals of youth are meagre, but it is in such simple experiences that character is formed and a treasure of happy memories accumulated. That for Longfellow it was a formative period, of earnest thought and feeling and real growth, his later correspondence plainly intimates. But the maturing of his mind was to be the work of a period still a few years in advance.

III

POST-GRADUATE DAYS

AFTER graduation, Longfellow made, in the autumn of 1839, a first essay in real life as teacher of a home school, conducted on the estate of a Southern gentleman, near Baltimore. About November 1st, he wrote, in Boston, a hasty note, *en passant*, to his friend Hale. "'I 'm off,' as the inhabitant of the mysterious mustard-pot said, on my way to Elk Ridge, Maryland, to take charge of a dozen or so boys, and live in the family of Mr. Daniel Murray." Here he remained a year, in a kindly, refined, and sensible circle, whose traits, habits, and modes of thought, contrasted as they were with those of the Northern people, interested him, and among whom he became much at home. The characters of these friends commanded his respect, and their kind ways won his attachment. It is strange that no reference to slavery occurs in his letters which remain, yet it would hardly seem possible that he was not in contact with it. Perhaps, however, his deep abhorrence and profound opposition to the institution in later days were begotten in him at this period, by a close observation of its evils and shames.

At the end of the year he decided to return home, notwithstanding pressing entreaties to remain. The school had grown much beyond its original numbers, and the task of discipline had become unpleasing to him. He was eager to return to Cambridge and to find his means of support in private tutoring. Yet he had experienced a disenchantment which usually awaits the returning alumnus. On June 5, 1840, he wrote to Hale from Philadelphia, on his way South: "Cambridge — shall I say it? — did not, after all, appear to me quite the paradise I had fancied. I did not feel quite so glad to get back as I had thought I should do. Ever since I left, I had looked forward with some hope of returning there for a year or perhaps more. It was the height of my ambition, when in college, to remain as a resident-graduate, and avail myself of the opportunities there so fully offered, of pursuing further and more thoroughly such general studies as my inclination prompted. The reason why the place appeared less charming is no doubt obvious enough. Class feelings and college feelings form so essential a part of the college student's life, and are so woven into all its pleasures, that a return under different circumstances could not but give things quite a changed aspect. Nevertheless, as I was asked to come back and take three or four little shavers to teach, I think, if I can arrange matters to suit at C., I shall say good-by to dear Mr. Murray next fall."

A month later he was still considering the matter, with the earnestness which a young man puts into these, to him, important life questions. " Whether it be worth a person's while to spend a year at Cambridge as resident-graduate I am not quite sure.   When in college I used to think it would be a kind of *Himmels-erde*, as you used to say. But I am afraid that a lazy man, like me, who should nominally devote his whole time to private, general study, would n't accomplish much ; some external force is needed, such as is supplied, in studying a profession, by the definite aim in view.   At any rate, I should prefer, in my own case, to have some regular engagement a part of the day."

That his thoughts were turning towards the profession which was the inevitable one for him is perhaps suggested in what follows : "I was amused," he says to Hale, "at your unchanged hostility to the Divinity School, as manifested in the appellation of ' monastic institution,' though,

to be sure, that is an improvement on 'Ortho-
pedic Infirmary.' Nevertheless, I was inclined
to agree with you in your views of the importance
of scientific theology. Think of the idea of 'dogmatic theology' in connection with the teaching
of Jesus Christ, who certainly, as he is the ex-
amplar of all Christians, is peculiarly such of the
Christian minister. I do not mean, of course, to
deny the need of an 'educated ministry,' nor to
suggest that the mere name and office will confer
an inspiration, rendering all else needless. Let
our clergymen continue to bring the best talents
and best educated talents to their work ; for
scarce any department of learning but may be
made useful as subsidiary to their profession.
But I cannot help thinking that the great deficiency of Unitarian preachers, which even Unitarians are beginning to see and acknowledge,
— their forgetting, apparently, that man has
a 'living spirit' as well as a thinking mind, —
may be in some measure traced to the course
of their studies in preparation for their office.
And, as you suggest, men placing so little stress,
as we rightly do, on mere doctrines and matters
of belief have something better to do than spend
much time on a technical divinity suited well
enough to the controversial divines of earlier
days. M. says he shall not study Hebrew be-

cause he will have the New Testament to preach
and not the old Jewish law. I am not sure that
he is quite right ; and, perhaps, Dr. Ware or
Dr. Palfrey would say the same, or something
stronger, of the idea which I have thrown out,
crudely enough, above. It seems to be evident
that new and more enlightened views are beginning to be taken of the true character and position
of the minister, and I should like to wait the
results. Perhaps it would only be waiting for
the river to run by."

After the momentary disenchantment which
he experienced on his return to Cambridge,
Longfellow found the years he spent there, after
college, much as he had previously imagined
them. They were evidently very useful and
happy ; his life conformed much to his natural
taste for quiet, and his disposition to follow the
bent of the hour in studying and thinking.

His pupils, regular or occasional, gave him
enough of stated occupation to prevent the list-
lessness he had feared without it, and for the
rest of his time he had abundant resources in his
love of literature and philosophy and in the
cultivation of his tastes. Music was, lifelong,
his unfailing resource. He enjoyed it in its
classical forms, and had a great love for simple
and expressive melodies. From Cambridge,

recourse was easy to the musical privileges of
Boston, and he constantly availed himself of
them. All other forms of art attracted an equally
appreciative attention. Even the exquisite per-
formances of that "living poem of motion,"
Fanny Elssler, the famous danseuse, gave him
intense pleasure.

Part of the time he was proctor, a college official the duties of whose office have never been
oppressive. The most exacting of them was attendance at daily prayers, morning and evening.
The jejune character of these exercises he notes,
yet sees the advantage and interest of a daily
assemblage of all the college. "After all, it is
not so much of a hardship," he says, "to get up
in the morning when a bell is ringing in your ears
two rods away; what I dislike is being tied down
to six P. M." One of his favorite enjoyments is
suggested in a note which he sends from the
Α. Δ. Φ. room to Hale in Boston. "What do you
think P. and I are doing in the Germanic way?
Reading Schiller's 'Räuber' o' nights. It is
somewhat raw-head-and-bloody-bones, — about
every other word being 'Hölle und Verdammniss,'
— with occasional touches of sentimentalism and
recollections of childhood and innocence on the
part of the robber-captain."

An occasional intimation of Longfellow's letters at this time begins to forebode that burthen of suffering and debility which became so important an element in his experience, and which weighed so heavily upon his ability to discharge the active duties of life. "The fact is, I have felt in the most miserable, wilted, incapable-of-mental-or-physical-exertion state all day long. This Indian summer may be very poetical and very good so far forth as it is an Indian summer, but its effects upon my bodily frame have been of the most disagreeable description. I felt too wretched to come in to the nights and suppers of the gods at Ryan's, where you are now enjoying yourselves. The best thing I can do is to go to bed.

"'Dear Damon, I am sick.'

"I am going, I know, to pass a miserable night; nevertheless, I am virtuous enough to wish you a good one."

Although only fragments of a desultory correspondence survive from this period, it appears singular that there occurs in them no reference to Longfellow's choice of a calling, and scarcely any to religious subjects in general. The reserve which was peculiarly characteristic of him may account for the latter. "The occasions are few," he writes, a little later, "when I can have such converse [upon deep themes], for it is impossible for me to speak of such things unless I am sure to meet with sympathy."

It may be that entrance upon the ministry was, for him, so natural a step, and so well understood among his friends, as to call for little particular mention. But even on the humanitarian and ethical side of his nature, some of the sympathies which were soon to show themselves most warm and controlling in Samuel Longfellow's mind had not been quickened in him at the age of twenty-three, nor had he awakened to some interests which were to seem to him among the most important. An incident which illustrates this is very striking, in view of the future development of his character. In March, 1842, a convention was called in Boston by Ralph Waldo Emerson, Amos Bronson Alcott, Maria Weston Chapman, and Edmund Quincy, — "a committee appointed at the Chardon Street Convention of October 28, 1841, to call a Convention for the public discussion of the credibility and authority of the Scriptures of the Old and New Testaments." William Lloyd Garrison was among those interested in this meeting, but he was detained from it by illness. The names of these persons are now a guarantee of the seriousness and dignity of purpose in which the meeting was called. But how it then appeared to our young resident-graduate, how little its aim or spirit appealed to him, are indicated in his letter to Hale of March 29th.

"I was getting ready to come into Boston this morning to make you go with me to the Convention, when I found by the 'Post' that it had adjourned *sine die*. I have seldom been more vexed, having made up my mind not to miss this, as I had done the others. I chose the second day as likely to afford the most fun, taking it for granted the first would be taken up with getting under way. There is no chance, I suppose, of these people getting together again; and it is a phenomenon, and, as you might say, a 'phase' of the spirit of the age, one does n't like to die without having seen. However, I expect to see funnier things yet."

But these were only the crude impressions of a youth reared under the highly conservative traditions of New England society; hitherto a student of books only; long cloistered in the academic seclusion of a college, and who had not yet found his real self. This immaturity was to yield quickly to the touch of real life, and to the stimulating influences which Longfellow was presently to encounter.

IV

THE DIVINITY SCHOOL : FAYAL

In the autumn of 1842, Samuel Longfellow entered the Divinity School of Harvard University. It was an epoch in his experience. He now took up, definitely, the serious work of life, after the somewhat dilettante interval of his resident-graduate years; he came under the influence of the Transcendental movement, then at its height, and he was to form the closest and most inspiring friendship of his life. Perhaps the latter, to one who had such a genius for friendship, was the most important condition of all in the development of his character and thought. After forty years of closest intimacy, Mr. Longfellow presented an estimate of Samuel Johnson in a brief memoir, and we need only refer to that for an apprehension of the qualities of a brave, talented, and faithful man and scholar, whose life and labors were quietly, and even obscurely, pursued, and have not yet, perhaps, been justly appreciated.

Johnson was a man of exceptional intellectual

power and brilliancy; of wide, thorough, and accurate scholarship; imaginative, introspective, rigidly conscientious; a typical transcendentalist in temperament and modes of thought. While Longfellow was calm, meditative, and debonair, social in disposition, and desultory in his habits of thought and study, his friend was austere, strenuous, systematic, and of tireless industry. An extreme individualist, Johnson's habits were naturally recluse. In dealing with debated questions he was dogmatic and aggressive. He shared with Longfellow a highly poetical nature; and his poems, while fewer, were even of a higher artistic quality and grander strain. The two friends were at one in the spirituality of their habitual thought, and their vivid apprehension of the facts and relations of the spiritual world. With Johnson, however, while his intuitions of divine things were, perhaps, loftier and more intense, they were rather by the avenue of the intellect. To Longfellow, these verities were known by that direct cognizance which is as spiritual vision. The latter was of much wider and warmer personal sympathies; more patient of opposition and of the slow response of their age to the truths with which they both yearned to enlighten and enfranchise it. But Johnson, also, was a tenderly loving son, brother, and friend ; a devoted pastor ; earnest, self-sacrificing, and practical in the promotion of social reforms. In moral fervor and firmness, and in the radical quality of all their thought, these men, so congenial to each other, were indeed " nobly peers."

The Divinity School of Harvard University at this time, as for long afterwards, was most meagrely endowed and equipped. Henry Ware, Henry Ware, Jr., and Dr. John G. Palfrey had but recently resigned. Dr. Francis and Dr. Noyes were in the charge of the school, doing, as Mr. Longfellow says, "the work of four professors." Of these very able and excellent men the former was an encyclopedic scholar ; refined, genial, and sensitive ; full of sympathy and help for any student who showed signs of real scholarship ; opening the stores of his own learning and the contents of his library, freely and kindly, to any such who sought his aid ; conservative in temperament and cautious in expression, but thought to be broader in his esoteric views than in his public utterances ; formal and reserved, yet cordial, in personal intercourse ; fluent but prosaic in his public offices ; a true gentleman and thoroughly a clergyman of the old school. Both he and his colleague were nearly fifty years of age.

Dr. Noyes, " the Rabbi," as he was affectionately called by the students, was a small, wiry, grim but good-humored man, probably the best Hebrew scholar of his day in this country; of quiet and even shy manners, but incisive in speech, and of a dry and occasionally caustic wit; rigidly upright; as an exegete and translator having no views of his own, but devoted with unqualified singleness of mind to identifying the meaning of his author. The lectures and recitations conducted by these good men were full of the best learning of their generation. They taught, or meant to teach, the youth before them to search for truth and nothing but the truth, fearing no consequences; but they belonged, especially Dr. Francis, to a former time; their methods were scholastic and antiquated; in later days, at least, their exercises were tedious and uninspiring in the extreme.

Among the students with whom Longfellow became associated in the different classes of the school was a full proportion of men who were to be eminent for learning, practical usefulness, or profound and progressive thinking. Of these, for him, Samuel Johnson was, of course, *facile princeps*. But there were others, in character, scholarship, power of thought, philanthropic zeal, and devotion to their calling, fully his peers. Joseph Henry Allen, Charles Henry Brigham,

Edmund Burke Willson, Thomas Hill, John Farwell Moors, Octavius Brooks Frothingham, William Rounseville Alger, Thomas Wentworth Higginson, Grindall Reynolds, were some of them. Johnson found the school "cold and spellbound," and it is likely that few of his fellow-students could follow his idealistic flights and "Transcendental Reveries." But where such men were gathered and at work, in all the warmth and earnestness of ingenuous, ambitious youth, there could hardly be a real stagnation and chill.

Yet they were all together, indeed, under the "spell" of their generation, which was only beginning to burst the fetters of traditional opinion and sentiment which hung heavily in those days upon the Unitarian community. A new learning had to be developed and justified before this emancipation should be accomplished. But the crisis was upon them ; the dawn of a genuine liberalism was breaking, and its rays were piercing the sombre evergreens about Divinity Hall. "The Transcendental movement . . . was then at full tide. The germs of it had been already in Dr. Channing's sermons. Dr. Henry had translated Cousin's 'Criticism of Locke;' Emerson had printed 'Nature' and the early addresses at Cambridge, Dartmouth, and Waterville, — this last his completest expression of spiritual pantheism, — and had collected and edited the chapters of ' Sartor Resartus ; ' Dr. Walker had given his Lowell lectures on Natural Religion, distinctly based on the existence in man of certain spiritual faculties which he held to be as trustworthy guides to spiritual truths as the senses and understanding are to physical facts." [1]

The young men had also found out certain German and French philosophers and mystics ; and in biblical exegesis were reading, beside the old stand - bys, DeWette's " Introduction " and Strauss's " Life of Jesus." They were going into Boston to hear Theodore Parker, who had secured his " chance to be heard " there, and was vigorously improving it.

At the same time, the inspiring tides of the antislavery controversy were surging throughout the land, washing away many prejudices and traditions besides those strictly germane to itself, and making men see all truth more clearly. The Texas debate and that over the Mexican War came on, and made politics exciting and bitter, yet infused into them a profoundly moral element.

All these influences expended themselves on the little community of the Divinity School, exciting endless discussions within and without the

---

[1] *Memoir of Samuel Johnson*, page 14.

lecture-rooms, stimulating deeply the minds and consciences of the students. Recitations were not seldom the scene of hot debates, in which the professors had to descend to the level of the combatants, and at times to act with some energy on the defensive. But, especially, controversy raged in the weekly debating meetings. "Do you still combat Willsonianisms on Friday nights?" Longfellow writes to Johnson, later. He was never an eager, nor even a willing, disputant; but he was singularly clear and firm in his convictions, which he expressed with positiveness and gravity, but preferably as intuitions rather than argumentatively. Unkind he could not be, yet he was not quite incapable of prejudices, in these early days, nor of something like partisanship, as his references to typical conservatives sometimes show. His opinions, thus far, were apparently little modified from those of the Unitarianism in which he had been brought up. But he was a radical and a transcendentalist by nature, and these traits were fast determining him to views in religion much in advance of the prevailing Unitarian thought. We can, even now, range pretty surely the partisans in those youthful discussions in Divinity Hall.

After a year of this new and stimulating life,

Longfellow seems to have found his health impaired, and he accepted an invitation to go out
to Fayal as tutor in the family of Mr. Charles
W. Dabney, long United States consul at the
Azores. That gentleman, by enterprise, force of
character, public spirit, and benevolence, had
become, as it were, a feudal chieftain on his
island. Surrounded by a large circle of his relatives and descendants, he lived with them a
charming life of refinement, bounty, hospitality,
and usefulness, in the midst of the half-tropical
loveliness and balmy atmosphere of (as Longfellow calls it in the words of some other) "the
green and breezy isle." Such a setting to existence, and the habits of such a family, were
thoroughly congenial to our student, and the year
was delightful and reinvigorating to him. His
duties were light, and of the kind which, with his
love of the young, he especially enjoyed. The
mild climate was very agreeable, and the picturesque scenery gratified his sense of beauty. Mr.
Dabney's family he called, in one of his letters
home, "the best in the world."

TO EDWARD EVERETT HALE.

HORTA, FAYAL, June 11, 1843,
Sunday Morning.

MY DEAR EDWARD, — Some of the family have gone to church this morning, but as I am quite satisfied, for the present, with High Mass, I consider it no loss to stay at home and finish my budget of letters.

We did not get away from Boston till Sunday, five weeks ago to-day. Saturday I was in town doing some last things, — I thought those last things would last forever, — and called at your door ; but ah ! with the thunder-word was it opened, ' He you seek has gone to Northampton.' I spared myself the pang of saying good-by again to your sisters, and wended my way to Howe's wharf and the brig Harbinger. Pleasant it was to me to find the memorial of yourself which you had left on the cabin-table ; most pleasant as your gift ; most pleasant, for thy sake, gentle Charles ! And let me add that you could not have made a better selection even had you known, as I almost fancied you must, how long and how longingly I had been watching a copy of Lamb's works on Mr. O.'s counter ; how " I had looked at the book and thought of the money and looked at the money and thought of the purchase."

The little note I did not find till (and it was doubly welcome then) one morning, after I had done being seasick, when I took the volume out of its envelope to read upon deck. . . .

As yet, I have picked up here only two little legends : one, that Columbus, in his early visits to these islands, was wont to stand for hours on the western shore gazing toward the setting sun, setting to rise upon Cipango and Cathay ; the other (and they evidently belong together, though I got them from very different sources), that there is on one of these islands, Flores or Corvo, the memory of a statue which once stood there with its finger pointing to the west. . . .

Don't let any of your friends persuade you, as some of mine tried to do (I did not believe a word of it, though, and so was not disappointed), that there is any *enjoyment* in a sea voyage. I deliberately declare that I did not have more than two hours of positive pleasure in the whole nineteen days. I was seasick, more or less, for a week, and, after that, so dull and listless, so guiltless of thought, feeling, or fancy, that it seemed as if I must have returned to that state of oysterdom in which, according to Dean Palfrey, I once learned patience. What would I have given, what would any one of us have given, for a hearty laugh ! I was not moved, either, by any sublimity in the ocean, and in this I was much disappointed. In fact, I think it needs to be seen from the shore, with a fine rocky foreground, or a strip of silver sand.

But it is time I told you something of the shore. On the morning of the 26th of May we rounded a rocky headland and saw the white, red-tiled houses and churches of Horta stretching crescent-wise before us, with a background of green cultivated hills. I reeled up the pier with Miss R. on my arm, and we were soon seated in Mrs. Dabney's comfortable parlor, sweet with the fragrance of flowers. How grateful it was! I have not yet commenced tutorial labors; indeed, the visit of the "Harbinger" is always *holiday*. We have amused ourselves, when it has not rained, by various walks through the town and excursions into the country. Everything is odd, foreign and picturesque. The most important excursion we have taken was our visit, last Tuesday, to the Caldeira, or crater, in the centre of the island. No longer ebullient, it has not even smoked within the memory of man. A large party we were, of ladies and gentlemen, on horses, donkeys, and feet. I found a walk of eight miles up a constant and very rough ascent, in the middle of a hot day, not a little fatiguing, and perhaps for this reason was little moved by

a scene which is expected, I believe, to put stran-
gers into raptures. In the midst of a steep and
barren common, covered with moss and heath,
you come, all at once, upon a huge cup, five miles
in circumference and perfectly regular ; so deep
that the sheep feeding at the bottom looked no
larger than white mice ; its sides channeled with
rains, and within it a gloomy Stygian lake and a
smaller cone and crater. The whole scene was
wild and gloomy, but had little beauty. Not so,
however, the Valley of the Flemings, which we
passed through at sunset on our return ; the
Happy Valley itself was not more lovely, — the
green hillsides and steep ravine ; the dark stone
bridge spanning the river-bed ; the white cot-
tages with the red-tiled roofs ; the villagers in
gayest dress, for it was a holiday; the church-
bell ringing and music of guitars from the houses ;
over all, the light of a summer afternoon. I
promise myself many a pleasant ramble through
this charming valley and many a trophy for my
sketch-book. Of churches and convents, of our
outdoor and indoor life, with family sketches,
such as I used to write from Elk Ridge, you shall
hear next time.

The following letter exhibits Longfellow's
extreme modesty, often in his early years ap-

proaching self-depreciation, which was a characteristic trait. His underlying self-confidence,
which made him so singularly firm in moral
decisions, appears at its close. But we have
here, chiefly, some of the struggles of introspective youth, and its transcendental musings.

TO SAMUEL JOHNSON.

HORTA, November 21, 1843.

I thank you, my dear Sam, for those beautiful
verses, your " Orphic Hymn," which breathes life
again into that dead fable, once indeed a living
symbol, as are all those beautiful myths in which
the poets — poets and prophets — of that fair
Grecian world shrined their wonderful truths.
Pray send me all your poetry. For myself, I
have scarce written anything of prose or verse
since I have been here — save letters. Indeed,
I have thought but little ; less, much less, than
I hoped and expected. Still, I have lived some
beautiful hours and had some revelations from
the world around me, — revelations which have
given peace to my soul and which I hope may
prove nourishing dews to the germs of spiritual
life within me. And yet, at times, — I cannot
help it, — I feel sad and depressed at the consciousness of my want of intellectual development. You cannot tell how much I suffered

when I first came here. I was very dull, and
silent, and stupid, and then much ashamed and
mortified at being dull, and stupid, and silent.
This made me very unhappy, more so than my
words convey. I felt as if I had nothing which
was wanted here. Then it was that, in my solitary walks, nature whispered, " Peace! vex not
thyself because thou art not as others! Be
content to be that which thou art; manifest thyself according to the laws of thy individual being.
The flower at thy feet hopes not to be a star, nor
strives to be aught but a flower. Be calm, and
fear not but thou wilt find thy place. Believe
that thou wast not for nothing sent into the
world. Obey thy nature, and fear not but that
thou wilt do the good thou wast sent to do."
Such lessons did the trees and rocks and waters,
the green hills and that calm, majestic mountain
breathe into my heart. Nor were words of man
wanting, and in the pages of Emerson I found
strength and reassurance. I am content now to
be silent when I have nothing to say. Indeed, I
begin to think silence better than words. What
says Goethe in this book before me? " We
constantly talk a great deal too much. I for my
part should be glad to break myself of talking
altogether, and speak, like creative nature, only
in pictures. That fig-tree, that little snake, the

chrysalis that lies there on the window quietly awaiting its new existence, all these are pregnant signatures; indeed, he who could decipher them aright might well dispense with the written or the spoken Amen!"

I cannot tell you how much comfort I have had from *one* source; how happy I have felt in the consciousness, as I never felt it before, of the near presence of friends absent in the body. Often, my friend, have you come and walked beside me in my evening ramble, or opened the door of this chamber, as you used to do that of my room in Massachusetts Hall, and this, not as a thing of fancy but a reality. "Spaces in Heaven," thus speaks Swedenborg, "are nothing else than external states corresponding to the internal. Hence, in the spiritual world, one person is exhibited as present to another, provided he intensely desires his presence, for thus he puts himself in his state."

TO JOHN T. G. NICHOLS.

HORTA, FAYAL, February 26, 1844.

DEAR JOHN, — . . . "Did you not promise to write to me?" I dare say I did, dear John, since you say so; but (if that be any excuse and not rather an aggravation) I had entirely forgotten it. My only wonder is that that dreadful sea voyage did not swallow up in its dull blank all remembrance of my former life. I had not, however, forgotten *you*, and when I read in your letter of all you are doing for the good of those about you, I felt as if I were leading here a very useless and inactive life ; and, what is worse, I felt as if I should never lead a very useful one ; for though I have the wish to do good, I have not the activity and energy of mind to plan and carry out benevolent objects. This is what discourages me in view of a clergyman's life, for as Dr. Johnson said, "I do not envy a clergyman's life because it is an easy life, nor do I envy the clergyman who makes it an easy life."

I have been interested in visiting the Catholic churches and witnessing their ceremonies. There is a sentiment of the poetic and a sentiment of the past hanging about them which appeals to my ideality and reverence. Still, it is very sad to see how dead and lifeless a shell these forms have become. The lower classes are sincere and devotional, but those who have such a degree of intellectual development as to see through and despise the form, without having spiritual development enough to put a new life *into* the form, are in bad condition. And this is the case with most of the " better class " of people here (particularly the men), and with some at least of the priests. If I could make a reform I would not begin by doing away with the Catholic religion, —for the mass of the people, at least. If one could reform the priests, and by that I mean as much as anything, open their eyes, now blinded by the dust which falls from every crevice of their ancient pile, and show them the mighty responsibility which rests upon them as the guardians of the people, and moreover show them *how* to begin a moral regeneration, that would be the best way. They do not object here to the reading of the Scriptures by the people, but the people, the poor, do not know how to read. They are improving, however, in this respect. Could I not get some Portuguese Testaments in Boston to distribute? Those who can read thirst for the word of God. . . .

TO EDWARD EVERETT HALE.

HORTA, FAYAL, February 17, 1844.

. . . I might tell you of the delightful October which we spent at Pico ; how we lived at " The Priory, " — which was a real priory, or had been ; how we slept in monks' cells and dined in the refectory ; how we jumped rope and danced Scotch reels ; how I read Lamb (your Lamb) and Bremer to the ladies and edited their newspapers ; how we bathed in the surf in the morning, and took long strolls in the afternoon, and virtuously read Portuguese in the evening ; how in short, we enjoyed ourselves as only people on the seashore can enjoy themselves. How often I used to think, This and this will I write to Ned Hale ; but the events which then filled all my horizon, and would have filled all my letters, are now crowded into a few lines, on the well-known principle of bridge-lamp perspective. . . .

This winter is only a cool summer. I find myself in somewhat improved health ; teach the three R's and such higher branches as are needed to docile pupils ; study Portuguese with a young padre in the Franciscan convent ; attend Catholic mummeries with poetic faith ; read the literature of the day, and enjoy my rest in the bosom of the best family in the world. But why tell you this ? Did you not yourself, years agone, in black silk kersey robes, foretell to me my present life in choice Ciceronian, whereof a document ever since remains in my portfolio, and furnishes me the very words ? "Mehercle, in campanis villis morari, in *hortis* splendidam prolem alentem, aut otiose in ora ambulantem et maris fluctus spectantem, tempus terere te oportuit." Imagine my delight in taking this out the other day ! . . .

HORTA, April 20, 1844.

MY DEAR MOTHER, — I am up early this fresh, glowing morning, and, after watering my garden, have come back to my chamber to send you word of my well-being, across the ocean on the wings of the morning. You are all asleep in the old home, for we have three hours the start of you. May your dreams be pleasant ones!

I am writing to the music of blackbirds and chaffinches, who are pouring out their song as if their souls were in it, touched by this summer sun. . . . The spring has come on, more beautiful than ever, and is not spring, but summer, crowned with glowing flowers, not pale snowdrops.

I wander about a good deal, regretting only that I have no companion, for the boys like better a ride on horseback. Occasionally I take my sketch - book, which is getting quite full, and which, one of these days, I shall have the pleasure of turning over with you and talking over with you. Sometimes we make up a party and take a long excursion into the country in the pleasantest possible way. Only, instead of the family wagon or the carryall, as in our excursions at home, we have donkeys, and servants to carry on their shoulders the great baskets of picnic good things, so that we make a much more picturesque appearance, winding up and down the steep roads, than the line of vehicles presents in which our parties convey themselves and their eatables to Black Point or Cape Cottage.

Since I wrote you, I have been to Castello Branco, and to the Caldeira again ; and last week Miss Green, Sarah Sawyer, Olivia Dabney, and I (the sole gentleman who could be mustered for the occasion), set off one glorious morning, and winding through my Beautiful Valley found ourselves at last in a deep rocky ravine, the object of our wanderings, and known as the laurestinus glen. A beautiful spot! The top is shut in by a sheer precipice a hundred feet and more in height, over which, when the river is full, pours the Salto Grande, or great waterfall ; but the waterworks here are like those at Versailles, which play only on particular occasions, that is, after a heavy rain. As it was, the water trickled down the face of the dark rock and dropped into a basin below with a cool, pleasant murmur. And here, shaded from the noon sun, we resigned ourselves to the romance of the time, and ate our oranges and bread. The sides of the ravine were covered with the clustered flowers of the wild laurestinus, and at our feet, in green nooks among the rocks, bloomed violets, " sweeter than the lids of Cytherea's eyes."

We get newspapers now and then by the whalers, so that we are not altogether ignorant of what is going on in the world at large of America. I cannot but wish, whenever a whaler comes in from New Bedford, that you had sent letters. I should welcome these brown-faced, rough-handed men, who sit beside me at dinner, most heartily if they brought me a letter now and then ; but when I ask them what news from America, and they answer, " Nothing particular," it seems to stop the conversation rather abruptly.

When the Styx was here a few weeks ago, engaged in a survey of the island, we saw the officers quite often. There was a party made for them at bagatelle, and another here. . . . After tea in the saloon, there were dancing and games, of which they are very fond here. The dancing always winds up with a Portuguese dance, a slow movement, accompanied by much snapping of fingers, castanet - wise, and very graceful when well danced. As everybody present is challenged and expected to join, I usually make my escape about this time. . . .

I long to hear what events are taking place in the family circle. Every night when I go to bed I look over the western hills and think of you, and I have been happy to find how near my friends at home have been to me in spirit since

I have been here. May God bless and guard you all, my dear mother! Remember me in your prayers.   With much love, yours,   SAM.

HORTA, May 7, 1844.

MY DEAR MOTHER, — . . . I am indeed thankful that my letters have brought me nothing but good news. I seldom dream of ill, yet it is not without some trembling of the heart that I watch the Harbinger slowly sweeping round the headland to her anchorage, or open the packet of letters which she brings. What a bitter winter you have had in New England! I am not sorry to have been away from it. I like cool and bracing weather; but that intense cold, which makes one's nose blue and fingers stiff, and seems to send all the blood back into the heart, is benumbing and contracting alike to body and mind. I like an atmosphere where I can expand and grow, as Mr. Emerson says, " like corn and melons."

I wish you had been here to breakfast with us on the first of May. We had none of the real mayflowers, nor any ramble in the woods before breakfast, because there are no woods to ramble in, but, that the day might not be unhonored, I went out early into the embowered gardens, and gathered for each plate at the breakfast-table a fragrant and dewy nosegay of damask roses, verbena, heliotrope, and sweet pea. The gardens are full of trees and shrubs and shady walks and nooks; but what strikes you most is the lavish abundance of the flowers, and their luxuriant growth. Walking out in the morning, you would think it had rained flowers all night. It was some time before I could learn to pick choice flowers with as little compunction or ceremony as if they were dandelions or buttercups, sure that to-morrow would repair the loss of to-day.

A bold style of gardening is practiced here which suits me. You transplant plants in full bloom, and they never mind it, but make themselves at home immediately. You stick down bunches of geraniums anywhere, and they take root without more ado and bloom in a month or two. And what do you think of cutting off the top of a great tree and setting out the *slip* (some twelve feet high, with all its branches on), and having it grow?

. . . I bathe in the sea almost every day, and walk in the afternoon after school one or two hours. One gets a great deal of exercise, too, out of a walk here, the roads are so roughly paved and so steep. I make great friends of the little boys who come begging for " cinc reisin," or five mills (a modest sum), with such merry voices and such beautiful eyes that I forget how ragged and dirty they are, and, in default of money, show them my sketches and try to talk Portuguese with them.   With love, affectionately yours,

SAML. LONGFELLOW.

In the autumn of 1844 Samuel Longfellow has returned from pleasant Fayal, and is again earnestly at work in his theological course.   He seems now to have taken up his abode with his brother Henry, who had married during his absence, and had acquired the fine old mansion in which he had had chambers since his first coming to Cambridge as professor, and which was destined to be his lifelong home.   Through the devoted love of the two brothers, it was, at intervals, the home, for long periods, of Samuel Longfellow also.

TO EDWARD EVERETT HALE (AT WASHINGTON).

CRAIGIE HOUSE [Cambridge], December 26, 1844.

DEAR EDWARD, — Here is one of those soft, mild, misty days that come, now and then, during our winter, to tell us that there is yet in the world such a thing as spring, and fill us with pleasant, nameless spring feelings and unpleasant, nameless colds-in-the-head.

Yes, we of the centre *are* " always writing dissertations," and the quantity of German books that I borrowed that week from Dr. Francis and the college library — and read, too, so far as I needed — would quite surpass belief. Really, though, I was quite glad to find how well I could push my way, without a dictionary, after two or three years' total abstinence. And this only confirms my belief that our college course does really amount to more than some people are fond of making out, and that, too, the old lamp can be rubbed up with ease and to some purpose. Now I am reading De Wette on Religion, with Frothingham and a dictionary, but our worthy professor's father-in-law, it must be confessed, is a little prosy, though very good.

My fire burning low, I got up to "put some:" and then, lying down on the too inviting sofa, finished my letter after a fashion to which I am greatly addicted, but which, pleasant as it is, hath this fatal inherent defect, that it avails nowise to the filling of blank pages or the satisfying the demands of expectant correspondents. Now I have but a page left and must tell what more I have to say in shorthand. I have been living a very quiet life here in Cambridge since my return ; seeing but few people out of Craigie House saving the Divinity Hallers. At the beginning of the year appeared at the school

one Greene, who has been through West Point
and the Florida War and the Baptist Seminary
at Newton, where I dare say you knew him. A
youth of keen mind, purely metaphysical ; before
whom, as fableth James Richardson, the whole
school did at once succumb and were led off into
the wilderness of Calvin-, or quasi-Calvinism.
To whom said James felt called upon to oppose
his whole energies, and with weapons of "the
innate holiness of man" and "no-such-thing-as-
sin," fight to the uttermost, — victory remaining
yet doubtful. All these things I look upon from
without. It was once said of Frank Parker that
he had been seen on the outskirts of one or two
Boston parties. I have actually been not on the
outskirts, but in the very midst and centre of
several, this winter. . . .

The vacation is coming near. I shall be for
the most part in winter quarters in Portland. I
wish they would let me preach. I feel curious
to know how I shall make out. . . . I have not
written a sermon yet, nor can I understand how
a man can write a proper sermon till he has
learned how by actual preaching.

The most important incident of Samuel Longfellow's remaining years at the school was the
somewhat remarkable one of his undertaking, in

conjunction with Samuel Johnson, to prepare a
new book of hymns for the use of Unitarian
congregations. The existing collections were
mostly very dreary. Dr. Greenwood's, compiled
about fifteen years before, was a great improvement on its predecessors, and was highly popular
in Unitarian societies, being in use in half or
more of them. But while it contained many
noble and beautiful hymns, it was encumbered
with a mass of sadly prosaic and antiquated ones.
Its doctrinal quality was, of course, that of the
conservative Unitarianism of the period. Several others were, about this time, coming into
competition with what may be called the standard collection. The motive which impelled these
young men to prepare yet another was largely a
poetical one, but it was still more the desire to
provide a body of hymns in which the religious
attitude of the worshiper should be that of a
more natural and immediate relation with the
Divine Spirit, and in which, especially, the dignity of humanity, the hopefulness of being, the
obligations of rectitude and brotherly love, should
have more adequate expression.

Once launched upon this enterprise, the two
friends prosecuted it with the greatest zeal and
thoroughness and with a business energy hardly
to be looked for in theological neophytes. They

read, criticised, and compared literally thousands
of hymns, — ransacking the collections of all
denominations, and the poetry of other languages
besides our own ; gleaning even in the newspapers, and utilizing portions of poems by skillful
adaptation.   They added thus to our resources
many new and beautiful hymns which have taken
a permanent place in our affections.   Whittier
they may almost be said to have introduced to
the world as a hymnist.   Newman's "Lead,
Kindly Light," they found in a newspaper,
anonymous, and so printed it.   The first word
and the second line were incorrect through a
misprint, and a more than doubtful change was
made by the young editors in the third stanza.
It is probable that Mrs. Adams's "Nearer, my
God, to Thee," here first appeared, at least in
an American collection.   Beautiful hymns from
Sears, Furness, Clarke, Harriet Beecher Stowe,
Emerson, Henry W. Longfellow, Trench, Very,
Lowell, and others, still fresh if not wholly new,
enriched the volume.   They diligently gathered
material, also, from private sources, and did not
fail in the courage it then required to invite contributions from Theodore Parker, printing his
noble "O thou great Friend to all the sons of
men," with one or two others from his pen.   A
number of the hymns were original, written by

the compilers themselves or by their friends, partly with a view to the particular aims of the new collection. Most, if not all of these, they published as anonymous, and not all have ever been credited to their authors ; but among them were some of the finest, which have remained among the treasures of our hymnology.

The " Book of Hymns " unquestionably marked a great advance upon its predecessors in poetical and spiritual quality, and it was in these respects that it was especially distinguished from them. While the tendencies of thought in the young men who prepared it, especially in Johnson, were radical and progressive, how moderate were their conscious departures from the Unitarianism of their day appears by the structure of this hymn-book and its particular contents. The hymns were classified under the headings " Jesus Christ," " The Christian Life," " The Christian Character," " The Communion," and the like. The supernatural character of Jesus is fully expressed by the titles " Saviour," " Redeemer," " King," and " Son of God," occurring throughout. Forty-four hymns refer to him particularly ; to Christianity and topics claimed as Christian, over two hundred more. " I am not sure," says Mr. Longfellow, " but this part was rather less the work of Johnson than of his collaborator, of whom he was generally a little in advance in his theology." But something was, after all, deficient, which the sensibilities of that distinctly "transition" period detected, and which was prophetic, doubtless, of the wider departures from Unitarian orthodoxy to which the minds of the young editors were tending. Many familiar hymns had been sacrificed to a new religious spirit which was making its appearance at this era. "Theodore Parker liked the book," says Mr. Longfellow in his memoir of his co-editor, because "it recognized more than was usual in the Unitarian hymn-books the idea that there *is* a Holy Spirit and that God is really present with and *in* the soul of man, a doctrine which Unitarianism then looked upon as somewhat fanatical."

On the whole, while the collection met with some severe criticism, and in few places superseded the well-established "Greenwood's," it received a gratifying welcome. An edition of five hundred copies was taken up in three or four months, the first society to adopt it being that of the Church of the Unity, just organized in Worcester, over which Longfellow's faithful friend Hale had just been installed. Theodore Parker's Music Hall congregation soon adopted it, and others followed. Within two years a second edition was called for, giving the editors a chance for revisions. Their correspondence during these years is full of their undertaking; its principles ; the business of it ; the criticisms on the book ; the changes and corrections needed.

TO SAMUEL JOHNSON.

[No date.]

" Now as to M. [a critic]. Our book is not thought *insignificant*, Sam. We get more talked about than any of the others. But M.'s objection is the funniest of all. The omission of certain *classes* of hymns might ' unfit ' a book for church use ; but how the omission of *particular* hymns can do so passes my understanding. Think of his taking the trouble to hunt up all those first lines ! I thought, at first, it was a long poem. But it is the best thing he could have done for us, Sam, if people will look at those hymns and think *why* we left them out. Our book needs to be compared with others to make its higher tone distinctly visible. . . . If they will but notice, in praise or blame, its *humanity !* "

But the editors excited especial criticism by their own alterations and amendments, although these were much less conspicuous in the " Book of Hymns " than they became in the " Hymns of the Spirit" of 1864. They defended these alterations on the practical ground taken, probably, by all compilers of church collections. Not long before his death Mr. Longfellow wrote to his successor in his Brooklyn pulpit, "It is the principle of *adaptation to a special use* which is the only justification of changes in hymns that I can offer. It is a question of using or not using which makes it needful to change (1) some verses originally written not as hymns, yet which one wants to use as such; (2) some hymns written by persons of different beliefs from those who are to use the hymn-book, phrases in which could not be conscientiously said or sung by the latter, yet which from their general value of strength, fervor, or tenderness could ill be spared. . . . If I had been making a collection of hymns or religious poetry for private reading, I should not have altered a single word."

It must be admitted that the liberty taken with individual hymns, especially in the "Hymns of the Spirit," was large. Colonel Thomas Wentworth Higginson, who was one of the original contributors to the "Book of Hymns," writes: "My sister, an intimate friend of Mr. Longfellow, satirized this propensity in one of the nonsense stanzas then so prevalent. It must be premised that as both the editors were named

Samuel, their book was often characterized as
the 'Sam-Book.' [1]

   "' There once were two Sams of Amerique
     Who belonged to a profession called clerique.
     They hunted up hymns and cut off their limbs,
     These truculent Sams of Amerique.'

"Longfellow entered heartily into this jest, and
illustrated the verses with a pen and ink sketch,
representing two young men with large shears,
cutting up rolls of paper. The likeness of Johnson, who was very handsome, with the air of a
high - caste Parsee or Assyrian, was unmistak-
able." [2]

[1] Or *Book of Sams.* Theodore Parker appears to have called
it so first.

[2] The same lady, in a poem characterizing, also, two of his
intimate associates, wrote these stanzas upon Longfellow, in
1847 : —

   "Thou, the gentlest and most youthful,
     With thy childlike poet-heart,
   And thy temper, trusting, truthful,
     Ignorant of selfish art;

   " Life's glad echoes, thrilling through thee,
     Woke the spirit to its tone
   As from harpstrings singing true, the
     Summer breezes wake their own.

   "And as such harp, in the woodland
     Hung to answer nature there,
   E'en beneath the storm wind's rude hand
     Swept with force, yields yet a prayer;

While the hymn-book engaged so earnestly
the minds of the two friends, especially Longfellow's, who seems to have done the larger part of
the work, the regular duties of the school were
proceeding, and their hearts were fully engaged
in them. The growth and maturing of Longfellow's character reflect themselves clearly in the
remains of his correspondence. His interest in
social reforms deepens visibly. His radicalism
of thought becomes more and more distinct,
although he parts slowly with the forms of opinion and modes of expression in which he had
grown up. The question of moral and intellectual fitness for the ministry agitates his mind,
alongside the anticipations of its various forms of
duty and visions of places of settlement, which
are common to students in the last year of their
theological course. There appears always that
mixture of extreme modesty as to his powers and
attainments, with the firmest quiet self-confidence
where a distinct moral or intellectual issue pre-

> " So thy spirit, answering duly
>   To each wandering zephyr's tone,
>   In its deeper chord, as truly
>   Vibrates back to Heaven alone."

" This image of the Æolian harp," says Colonel Higginson,
"an instrument much more familiar fifty years ago than now,
is perhaps the best description of the temperament of Samuel
Longfellow."

sents itself, which was characteristic of the man throughout life. Among the particular personal influences to which he was yielding, at this time, was evidently that of Theodore Parker, whose boldness of thought, the naturalness of his religious attitude, and his simple, earnest piety, attracted Longfellow; while something in his temper, his disposition to satire, and his occasional truculence repelled the younger man. As the champion of freedom in religious opinion, and the martyr of the moment to that principle, Longfellow was now wholly in sympathy with him, as he was beginning to be with Parker's more peculiar views. "Yes," he says, in writing to Hale during the winter of his middle year in the school, "I have actually got through my letter without mentioning THEODORE. You have heard from Boston, I suppose, how they are stewing about him, with Clarke-exchanges and Sargent-resignations and Church-of-Disciples-secessions and Christian World and Register scoldings. Let every man be fully persuaded in his own mind, but I am afraid the Unitarians are going to be false to their great principle and the ground they have taken and been preaching ever since the Unitarian controversy."

TO SAMUEL JOHNSON.

CAMBRIDGE, December 19, 1845.

DEAR SAM, — . . . I wonder if you have been enjoying these spring days as I have? It is an intense delight to me, an intoxication just as in the real spring. . . . I have just had a visit from ——, but it did not do me much good. He seems to be living in a great excitement; as he says, "preaching Pantheism, Parkerism, and all sorts of heresies," — but I should rather see a self-devoted, quiet earnestness. Yet why demand of all the same fruits? He is evidently arousing his people, and putting into them new life, which a calmer man might fail to do. It is not the highest state, but may open a way for it. I will not quarrel with a living spirit, but pray that it may gain depth. . . . To-night there is a discussion at the Hall, adjourned from one on Wednesday, when your Infidelity resolutions were discussed. They take up also the question of "ministerial fellowship" with those who teach only "Love to God and Man." But I will not tell you any more of these things till you come. Don't fail, unless you are happier at home. I have some new poems to read you, not very great but pleasing, by Chenevix Trench. . . . I am physically ill at ease to-night, and cannot write you to any purpose but to say that I am thinking of you.

TO EDWARD EVERETT HALE.

CAMBRIDGE, April 15, 1846.

DEAR EDWARD, — Your note came yesterday, with the hymn, which I am very glad you sent me ; for I recognize it as an old favorite which I used to hear sung at home years ago, but which had quite slipped out of my memory. Thank you for interesting yourself in our book. Your various notes would not have remained unacknowledged, but that, the whole of the last week after you left me, I was utterly busy in reading up for and writing a dissertation for Dr. Noyes on the different explanation-theories of the Temptation. I dare not tell you of the Studien and Kritikens, and Eichhorn's Bibliothek and Leben-Jesu's, that I dived into ; suffice it to say the dissertation was written and read, and I am free for a time from such like. . . . About your Ordination Hymn. In part for the reason above mentioned, I have not written a word of it. But I will proceed immediately to put my brain in motion that way. I did fashion a verse or two of it, rudely, as I walked over the bridge one day ; but have quite lost them. Perhaps I shall pick it up as I walk into town to-day. You shall have it as soon as I can write it, for better, for worse. But if your choir are in haste, don't make them wait for my uncertain muse.

Most of all, in writing this, I want to thank you for your warm-hearted note about my sermon. I am heartily glad that you liked it, and that you wrote me all that you did and just as you did. It was and will be to me a great encouragement, to know that anything I have written has met so ready and real sympathy from you ; that sermon in particular, which I *did* write from a depth of feeling that gave me a confidence of its essential truth. I am very glad that you felt it, too. For myself, ever since I wrote that, I have felt more and more strongly that we need a more living faith in Jesus as a *personal reality* to us, not an abstraction ; not a religion or system of truths ; not a passive organ of the Infinite Spirit, but a living, human friend ; one who grew in grace ; was made perfect through suffering ; whose life is to be interpreted by our own deepest, holiest experience. Such a view, I am convinced, will make him to our souls at once more perfectly human, more truly divine ; more perfectly natural, more profoundly supernatural ; and, so far from diminishing, will but deepen and quicken our reverence, as well as our love, for him.

At length the momentous experience of a first public appearance in the pulpit.

TO SAMUEL JOHNSON.

CAMBRIDGE, January —, 1846.

DEAR SAM, — Your beautiful letter came not till Wednesday morning. Sam, it did me great good. I hope one day to reach such earnestness of resolve and purpose, myself. It was precisely what I hoped this first preaching would do for me, but you must have seen that it did not — has not yet done so. I need, how much, to be roused to an earnest, practical love of man. I believe it is in me, Sam, if it can be kindled; this must be my prayer; this must be your prayer for me. I feel that it will come; voice after voice calls in me, Lord Jesus, come quickly!

TO SAMUEL JOHNSON.

CAMBRIDGE, Monday, January 19, 1846.

DEAR SAM, — I have preached, and like it very well! But the strangest thing must come first; strangest because it was least of all expected or premeditated; yet came about in the most natural manner. I am to preach next Sunday for Theodore Parker, at West Roxbury, which society, it seems, he still supplies (preaching there himself in the afternoon) till February. So you see that I have quite got the start of you in that matter. . . .

But first about Dedham. You know the melancholy storm on Saturday. I went to D. in the evening train, and, getting out of the cars, soon encountered a little man whom I knew at once must be Dr. Lamson. I introduced myself, and we trudged up through the snow to his warm house, where I was in five minutes entirely at home, so informal and kind were they. . . . We sat up till eleven o'clock, talking. But, oh ! Sam, all night I dreamed haunting dreams about my first preaching. I cannot remember them now, but one was that when I got into the pulpit I found that my sermon was entitled Lalla Rookh, and I was afraid to preach it. The last phase of the dream was that I awoke and went down, and found that it was six o'clock of Sunday *evening;* that I had, in fact, slept all day, and that the doctor had preached in my place !

After breakfast I selected my chapter and hymns. The doctor's collection proved to be the old " New York Collection," unlike any I ever saw, and I could not find one of the hymns I wanted, except " While Thee I seek," for the opening in the afternoon. The sexton came for the hymns, the bell rang the knell (of parting Sam), and we went through the snow to the church. To my great joy it had cleared off and was a glad, bright sunshine. At the head of the broad aisle (which is a short one), the doctor bowed to me to go up on one side, while he ascended on the other. We went up the pulpit stairs like Moses and Aaron, " in the sight of the congregation," which consisted, as it seemed to me, of about *ten* people. I suppose the real number was fifty or so. I would have waited for more to come, but presently the doctor, who knew better, motioned to me to begin, and I arose and made the opening prayer. It seemed just like the School. Then I stepped down and would have taken the hymn-book, but the doctor told me the Scripture must be read next. (N. B. I had been studying the order of the services all the morning!) So I opened the Bible, and made no blunder, except reading the wrong chapter, mistaking xviii. for xvii. The long prayer I made myself, and made it short, I suspect. Then, the sermon. I was not in the least embarrassed or nervous, but felt rather stiff and not altogether at ease ; moreover without a spark of enthusiasm. I was glad to find that I could see the people, and I discovered one young man listening intently. . . . But in the afternoon I looked and he came not. Sam, the sermon of " Suffering," I am sorry to say, moved rather heavily. In the

afternoon I gave them the sermon of " Reforms."
I felt now entirely at my ease; the discourse is
more animated and I was myself quite lively. At
its close the doctor said quite heartily : " I like
your sermon very much. I should not wish to
alter a word of it." So ended my first preaching ; and on the whole I liked it very well, as I
said. Still, I felt no seriousness or solemnity
about the matter, *that* I must tell you. In the
prayers, indeed, I did at times lose myself and
felt something of earnestness. I found not the
least difficulty or fatigue in speaking. It must
be a remarkably easy church to speak in, and I
am glad you are going to begin there. In the
evening we went to hear Theodore give a discourse on slavery. It was vigorous and direct,
and roused me a good deal. It had reference to
the duties of the North upon that matter and its
interest in it. There was a good deal of irony,
some sarcasm, and a hit at the Boston Association of Ministers. Sam, I cannot quite like that
man. I feel that we are not of spiritual kin.
After the lecture, Dr. L. introduced me to Theodore, who inquired if I were engaged the next
Sunday. I said I had not intended to preach
that day. Then he asked me to preach at West
Roxbury, and I told him I would, if he wished.
So we shall be near each other, Sam, and in the

afternoon I shall walk over to Dedham and spend
the night with you at Dr. Lamson's. At parting
the doctor gave me one dollar. Theodore says
he pays ten dollars !

The genuineness of Longfellow's sentiments
is intimated in his disappointment at the effect
on himself of his early essays in preaching, the
importance of which, as spiritual experiences, a
sincere beginner naturally magnifies in his youthful anticipations, not realizing that these first
occasions must needs be matters of form, largely.

TO SAMUEL JOHNSON.

PORTLAND, February 17, 1846.

DEAR SAM, — Coming home to-night I found
your letter ; most welcome, the only word I have
had from your region of the world since I left
Massachusetts, which, indeed, is only nine days,
though seeming many more. . . . I never know
what any experience does for me, except when I
find that I can *do* something which once I could
not ; then I know that I have grown stronger.
I did expect, as I told you, that this preaching
would be an era to me, but it has not proved so
exactly, and so I am content to "expand and
grow like corn and melons." The want that I
feel is still devotional feeling, depth and warmth

and earnestness of religious feeling. I have written nothing since I have been here; have preached once at S. . . . You know what a stormy Sunday it was; I had to walk half a mile to church, . . . and had fifty people to hear me — my usual audience! A few more, I thought, in the afternoon; but the music, Sam! It is truly a most essential thing to the clergyman. I had to cut down all the hymns as much as possible, and, from the first one, "Father, Thy paternal care," they themselves gave me the hint by dropping off the last verse, of their own accord. I was only too glad they did. Such melancholy and unheard-of tunes! . . . I added two pages to my "Spiritual Aid" sermon, and preached it in the morning, by way of variation. In the afternoon, I gave them the sermon of "Suffering," and Sam, *I* liked it very much, whatever they did. You cannot say that I depreciate myself; I do not, unless I compare myself to somebody else, and then I cannot but do so. It was revealed thus to me that I could preach better, more fervently, in the afternoon than forenoon.

I had one new experience at S.; being asked to "say grace" at table and to lead the family prayers, which last I like to do. By the way, I thought it strange that neither at Dr. Lamson's nor Theodore's did they appear to have family prayers. . . .

Sam, when I said that I liked my sermon, I meant that I felt there were truths in it, and so expressed that they must reach, and perhaps help, some hearts. If it could but draw any nearer to Jesus! . . . I have begun the Life of Henry Ware; it is very simply presented, and I know I shall yet get good from it. I find already something of my own experience and my own traits of character in it, and this encourages me to think that I may become a serious, earnest, fervent, helpful preacher. You may depend upon it, for some minds at least, the thing needed is to be brought into actual contact with men and women and children. *Your own* men and women; *your own* vineyard. Some people seem to have an intense desire to meet certain wants of the community, the age; my sphere I feel will be to meet the wants of individuals.

TO SAMUEL JOHNSON.

PORTLAND, August 20. 1846.

DEAR SAM, — Last night came your little note instead of yourself. I have been looking daily for a word from you, saying when you would be here. I am very sorry it is not to be at all this vacation; but there will be time yet, and Cape

Cottage will wait for us, you know, and the sea,
ebbing and flowing every day till we come again.
I went over to the cape last Wednesday, and
spent three happy days. Glorious sky, sea, sunshine! There I found my classmate and old
friend J., who is gentle and poetic and musical,
and that was very pleasant for me. Some of the
Thaxters, too, from Watertown, but not Levi,
nor John Weiss, who are both secluded on a
little lighthouse rock among the Isles of Shoals,
off Portsmouth. There they found an eremite,
a Mr. Laighton, formerly a politician, but now
retired from the strife of that unholy life, with
his books, into the quiet of the lighthouse, the
only habitation on the island. Wentworth [Hig-
ginson] arrived the same afternoon at the cottage, where his mother and sister already were,
and altogether we enjoyed, in the quietest way,
the luxury of breathing the breath of life, and
doing nothing for the good of the human race,
— a beautiful " Typee " life. We bathed ; we
sat on the rocks, holding books in our hands, but
not reading ; we watched the surf ; we counted
the white-sailed boats and ships that all the time
went to and from the town, which was just out
of sight behind a turn in the coast. We sat
under trees, singing, or weaving chaplets of bay-
berry leaves ; we repeated snatches of sea-ballads

—all the various employments of "him whom the world calls idle." Upon the top of a beautiful cliff crowned with pines and birches, I planned a little book for people to take with them to such places, which should contain all the charming bits of poetry in the language about the sea and the seashore. You must help us from your stores.[1]

A little hymn-book has lately been published here in Portland, which is vastly more "profane" than ours, for it contains bodily "Oft in the stilly night," and "Isle of beauty, fare thee well." . . . On Sunday Dr. Nichols begged me to preach in the afternoon. I chose my sermon on "Coming to Christ," the divine in us recognizing the divine in him. I know not how its "transcendentalism" was liked. Have you ever seen Dr. Channing's sermon on the "Imitableness of Christ's Character"? He says, "Christ never held himself up as inimitable, unapproachable, but directly the reverse," "nor is there anything

---

[1] This was the origin of *Thalatta*, in writing which he was assisted by his friend Higginson, who says : "In literature, he had his brother's delicate taste, with an even finer spiritual perception. His preparation of *Thalatta* was a work of art ; the arrangement of the poems was by their themes, and had an order of its own. The book was the child of his youth, and he never ceased to love it. All his life he was collecting materials for a second edition, which never came."

in him of which we have not the promise, the principle, the capacity in ourselves." "He is truly our brother." I found it here, and liked it much.

V

WITH the summer of 1846 student life is ended, and the agitating and often weary period of "candidating" begins. Mr. Longfellow had already appeared in several pulpits, and it was still early winter when, after preaching there several Sundays, he received a call to West Cambridge. He declined, however, to be permanently settled, but accepted a temporary engagement.

The following letter is headed by a clever pen and ink sketch of the village and church of West Cambridge.

TO SAMUEL JOHNSON.

WEST CAMBRIDGE, November 9, 1846.

DEAR SAM, — Do you want to see my church at West Cambridge? Here is a distant view, which I sketched on my walk up yesterday, on the back of my sermon on spiritual realities. A glimpse between two great elm trees, a cloudy morning, with gleams of sunshine lighting up the white houses against the dark blue hills. I preached my old sermon of the reformer's aims. And now, Sam, farewell to reform sermons! I am not yet calm, and high, and pure enough myself, I feel, for this. I can but protest and complain ; and this, I feel, is out of place in the church. I came away yesterday afternoon restless and dissatisfied and unhappy ; not more serene, devout, and cheerful, as these hours in the sanctuary should have made me ; and can I hope my people were any better off ? . . .

I have six or eight manuscript hymns, some of which you have seen. . . . Do let us have some more *original* ones ; such as will embody the true ideas, without all the plague of altera- tion ; such as will just suit our sermons. I wish we had done this at first, instead of altering old hymns. Take your sermons, Sam, and write a hymn for each one. This was the way Dod- dridge made his book. . . .

To-day I voted, for the first time in my life, and for Palfrey as representative to Congress. I have been reading some facts about the war to-day, and it is lamentable to see how those weak Whigs, all but sixteen in both Houses, were panic-stricken, frightened, cajoled into as- suming and supporting the war, — a cunning trick of a despotic President, who first assumed a power to which he had no shadow of claim, and then duped Congress into taking the thing off his hands. It seems that they need not have done anything even to rescue Taylor; first, because any assistance from them must necessarily be too late, and secondly, because he already had authority to demand aid, as he did from Louisiana and Texas. Here is a thing to be reached by political action. Mr. Webster says, in that weak speech of his: "If the voting for the war-bill stained a man's hands with blood, then is the whole Whig party red with blood up to the chin." True, O Daniel! Think of it! Only sixteen men straightforward enough to cut through a "complicated question" by a simple fidelity to conscience, — not even acute politicians enough to keep out of this trap of their opponents!

TO EDWARD EVERETT HALE.

CAMBRIDGE, December 15, 1846.

DEAR EDWARD, — I admire the vermilion edict,[1] and to hear would be to obey; but it is *not* "ceteris paribus" (if one but knew the Chinese for that!), and now, while you are packing your portmanteau, I will tell you why I cannot

---

[1] Hale had left a note written upon a sheet of red paper, used by the Chinese as a visiting-card.

come.   Because I am going to West Cambridge
on the 2d of January, to take up my abode and
supply the pulpit for three months. . . . It is
rather a bleak time to go to so rural a place, but
I weary of wandering about and seeing new
faces every Sunday, and "getting the hang" of
a new pulpit every week. . . . I am glad you
have spoken a good word for our hymn-book. . . .
Though the people of New Bedford spoke kindly
of its poetry, none of them seem to have seen
the real merit of the book in its higher, health-
ier, more active, love-to-man tone ; in short, its
more purely Christian tone.   Dr. Ephraim Peabody showed some insight into the book and our
views.   Remorse for sin is not there, and was
not meant to be.   Not that it is not a real, sometimes terribly real, state of soul, but surely not a
healthy one ; and surely, too, a most private and
individual one, and (even if one should find a
sincere and earnest expression of it in verse) out
of place in *public* worship. . . . Of course, we
look for likers of our book rather in new pulpits
than in old.   Sunday before last I was at Mount
Pleasant, in an elegant, but rather desolate
church, with an unequaled expanse of pulpit.

TO SAMUEL JOHNSON.

NEWBURYPORT, January 18, 1847.

Bless you, Sam, and a happy New Year to you. You will see by my date that I have accepted the invitation of the First Religious Society to preach for them one Sunday and make a little visit. The place looks forlorn these cold days, so chilled and blue-nosed! The people, though, are only too attentive, and will have me to dinner, or to ride, or to call, or to tea, or at least to be introduced to them on the meeting-house steps. The young ladies beg me to come to their Sunday-school class, and the school committee will take me into the young ladies' Academy, where I shall be called upon for an address. Sam, a young minister must keep clear of these girls! Beautiful enthusiasts, in vain will all the P——s strive to tame their efflorescence! There is a picture of the whole matter in Retsch, — the poet in the hands of the water-nymphs.

The first thing that caught my eye on entering the pulpit was a bunch of flowers; so I read "Consider the lilies," but as I brought them home the bitter air froze them into "poor, unsightly, noisome things." I was glad to find they came from a married lady. . . . My former landlady at West Cambridge was sad when I left, and begged me not to preach my best sermons here. About this society C. wrote me that they need a reformer, one who would cry aloud and spare not. The committee who came to see me would n't allow but what all was in an excellent state, as if only to the righteous was a minister to go. The gentleman with whom I took tea last night said, in the elegant language of Ezekiel, that they wanted a minister who would make a " shaking among the dry bones ; " that they wanted some one "to preach up sin !" Can I do that, Sam ? Would n't it be as well to preach it *down ?* I can't understand, nor will I yield to, this morbid desire of some people to be made uncomfortable. If they know they are sinners, as they say, why want to be told so by their minister? I can, however, understand how people may desire to be aroused from inaction and indifference. But I don't like this depending on the minister for excitement ; this passive waiting to be moved. Some of the people here evidently want evangelical preaching. "Such preaching as Peabody's and Parker's and Putnam's," said my abovementioned friend. How liberal ! thought I ; this is the right sort. But I found he meant Nathan Parker of Portsmouth, not Theodore.

TO SAMUEL JOHNSON.

WEST CAMBRIDGE, March 2, 1847.

DEAR SAM, — I shall never ask you to come and see me again, I believe! I felt so lonely and downcast after your departure. I sought in vain to take refuge in a sermon. In the afternoon I felt as if a good walk would revive me, and I went away down to the two elms. Then I called in to see an old lady, very sick, who lay panting for breath upon her bed. I could say but little to her, and I felt that, at such a time, the voice of prayer was the most calming and strengthening thing. Two days after, she died, and to-morrow I attend the funeral. Next, I stopped to read one of my sermons to a poor woman who has been confined to the house for sixteen years, and then home, in just such a sunset of fine pale gold as we saw the trees against, the other afternoon. The evening was spent in futile attempts to fix my mind upon a text and a sermon. So I resolved to get an exchange, and stopped at Briggs's, Thursday, on my way to Brookline, but found no one. The night with Sam Eliot, who was preparing his "Words of Christ." They urged my preaching for them on Sunday, and I went over to effect an exchange with old Dr. Pierce, but found him not at home, and proceeded to Boston. There, after dinner, I went to the South End after Waterston, who was kindly, but had promised to be at home on Sunday. Then away to the North End to Robbins, who would gladly, but could not; then to Dr. Parkman's, who was engaged at Old Cambridge, but would prefer West Cambridge, only, being sick, wanted if possible to stay in Boston; expressing at the same time deep concern for my dilemma, and tempted to say he would go. This failing, I went to tea with Miss Dabney, and told her I had a good mind to take passage in the Harbinger, next week, and indulge myself with a voyage and a recruiting visit in Fayal till the autumn. The night at Craigie House. Friday, an attempt upon Divinity Hall, but Wentworth Higginson was engaged at Newburyport, and nobody else at home. So into Boston again. Dr. Parkman had arranged with Winkley, but was still anxious to go for me, only for his erysipelas, and the prospect of a stormy Sunday. Met Weiss with a lame eye, seeking, like myself. Went off to J. F. Clarke, — not at home. Then away down beyond Boylston Market to Fosdick, but he wanted an exchange for only half a day; so I lost the enviable chance of appearing in Hollis Street ! Then to J. I. T. Coolidge, who was not at home; again met Weiss, forlorn;

Muzzey must be at home; Barrett had his Communion. Finally, at three o'clock I took the Lowell cars for Medford, sure of Caleb Stetson; but ah! he had promised to preach a famine sermon, and so the last stay was gone, at four o'clock Saturday afternoon, except myself, who must now needs be at home. So, through the snowstorm, I took my way to West Cambridge, no longer discouraged, but quite sure, now, that all would come out right.

After tea I took up an old school essay (known to Frank as " Metamelomai," — I repent), and after copying the first page, launched off into a new vein, and (with an interlude in the parlor), at eleven o'clock stopped at the end of the fourth sheet, determined not to sit up any longer. The sermon turned out a sort of reform discourse: " Repent, — the cry of the prophet of all ages." I was glad to find that, in preaching, it seemed quite long enough. Sunday morning came, with its slush. Then the rest of " Metamelomai," with a few new pages, must make the afternoon sermon, more personal than the morning's. And so ends this true history of a young minister's travels in search of an exchange. Do communicate to Frank the final end of " Metamelomai;" it will amuse him.

On the conclusion of his engagement at West Cambridge, Mr. Longfellow was pressingly besought to remain as permanent pastor. But, while he found it hard to do so, he adhered to his resolution of postponing settlement until he had had the experience of preaching in a greater number of parishes. Some of the tokens of regret at his departure were quite affecting; one was very handsome. "I have not written my [last] sermon yet," he says to Johnson, "and shall not give them any *farewell*. I hate scenes, and am shy of emotion now. When I feel it coming on, I make myself rigid against it. I used to be too sentimental. Sam, the ladies have given me a beautiful gold watch as a remembrance. What *can* I say but *je reviendrai ?*"

In the autumn of 1847, their kind insistence still troubles him. "I went to West Cambridge last week and spent a day and night in making visits to former friends. Sam, they want me still. S. said so directly, and that they wanted but a word from me to give me a call. I am rather sorry. It seems not to leave me free. Ought I to yield to this entreaty? Sometimes it seems so. Yet I still feel as if I might find a place more truly *mine*. W. is staying there, and is to preach one Sunday more. It is hard if their regard for me prevents them doing justice to others."

While he was at West Cambridge, Mr. Long-fellow had received a similar earnest call to Newburyport. The uncertain state of his health chiefly decided him against what he felt would, or should, be a laborious field. The same cause led him, on leaving West Cambridge, to take an interval of rest from professional work, and to resort to a water-cure, then the popular nostrum. But he yielded to a tempting invitation to preach a few Sundays in Washington, and to enjoy its balmy climate, before proceeding to Brattleboro' for the hydropathic treatment.

TO SAMUEL JOHNSON.

WEST CAMBRIDGE, March 22. 1847.

DEAR SAM,—The deed is done ! Yesterday Mr. Dorr read to the Society my letter declining their invitation, and saying that, on account of my health, I should not think of being settled anywhere at present. Sometimes I feel ashamed to say anything about my health, when I think how many much sicker persons than I are faithfully working away in the ministry. But when I think how much better I can take the time now than ever again, and how much more good it will do now, I feel that I have not done wrong, and that in a few months I shall be able to be strongly and satisfactorily at work. It certainly looks morc like cool judgment than enthusiastic self-devotion to God's work. Alas, Sam, that baptism has not yet come to me! . . . The W.'s, to whom I had confided my determination, pleaded to the last, and Mrs. W. in this touching manner. I had been reading her some verses of Isabella Batchelder's, called " Jesus knocketh," and the next morning I found the following appended in pencil : —

> "Jesus knocketh, when his people,
> Orphaned by the hand of God,
> Call thee as his faithful servant
> To divide to them his word.
> Jesus knocketh ; oh ! refuse not
> Pastor, friend, and guide to be ;
> Cheer the fainting ; win the sinner ;
> Jesus waits ; He calls for thee."

I hated to resist their entreaties, but I did. The W.'s are still desirous that the Society shall await my emergence from the *Wasser-Kur.* But I will not promise them to come, even then.

I have not told you of my visit to Plymouth. I stayed until Tuesday morning, having a very pleasant time. Finest weather ; clearest sky ; bluest sea ; how it made my heart bound ! The church is Gothic, under the loveliest avenue of old elm-trees. Old Dr. Kendall, a kind-hearted, liberal man, like Dr. Flint, had me to tea ; and a mile out of town, in a sunny valley, I found my pleasant, enthusiastic, transcendental farmer friend, Ben Watson, living in a cottage which I planned for him, and which turns out as comfortable and convenient as it is pretty. He is a real worker, and by and by will have a lovely place ; as yet, all is to be made ; but he is one who can live a good while on ideals. . . .

Plymouth is really an interesting place. You are terribly disappointed in the Rock, which you can scarcely see in the midst of the wharf. But the upper half, which lies now in front of Pilgrim Hall, I looked at with a good deal of emotion. But the burial-hill and the sea ! The heads of the people are full of free thought, excited on all reforms. It is a great place for freedom, as it should be with that sea and those recollections. There is even the social freedom of going into each other's houses without knocking. I fear the railroad will do away with much of its primitive character before long.

R. has sent me his discourses on theology, supernaturalism, etc. Quite characteristic, and loosely enough stated, but containing good truths, plainly told, about the relations of God, man, and Jesus. He takes the ground that, since Nature is God, nothing can be really supernatural, but only above our present knowledge of Nature. Christ was profoundly natural, etc., after the fashion of the Dudleian Lecture [Dr. Furness's]. This is the great thing to be taught now, and I am glad R. has said it.

TO SAMUEL JOHNSON.

PHILADELPHIA, May 2, 1847.

DEAR SAM, — Your letter came welcome to me in Washington, and you have wondered why the oracle gave no response. Truly the god was doing what the Jewish prophet cast into Baal's worshipers' teeth about him, walking, eating, sleeping, going of journeys. With no great business on hand at Washington, I was idly busy, and had no quiet place where to write comfortably. I was there just three weeks and two days, and like Washington vastly better than from former experience I supposed I should. First of all, meeting the spring, with its soft air and green grass, and budding, blooming trees, was a separate joy and delight of itself. The grounds about the Capitol were my especial resort while I lived near by, as I did the first week. Then, after I went to the other end of the city to stay at my uncle's, I used to walk among the hills which "stand about" the city and lead you over to Georgetown, and drink in new life, and gather violets and sabbatias and saxifrages under the trees, after a manner that would have made

Margaret's and Mr. Judd's heart glad. After
all (it was thus I meditated as I sat on a tree-
root and picked the rose-colored flowers), we owe
much to the man who gives us feelings and
images that come up to us in our pleasantest
hours. This was apropos of Margaret's walk
through the woods, which came to me in those
pleasant Georgetown walks. Sometimes, seeking the shadow, I tried a sketch, and I will show
you a little picture of one pretty spot with a
veritable ruin in the foreground. But I did not
feel any better in Washington. . . .

It is the strangest place externally, full of
huts, hovels, and barren, gullied commons, in the
midst of handsome houses and grand public
buildings. Under that sky I felt some of the
real beauty of the Greek architecture. Morally,
the people are rather indolent than anything else,
I should think. I mean the permanent society,
but there is such a vast floating population that
there is no *tone* of general sentiment, and the
place is fearfully corrupt. The whole class of
yellow people, many of the women of which are
pretty, are at once victims and cause of one portion of this corruption. I did not get at much
about slavery. In the city the colored people
are mostly free, generally degraded, but have
schools and churches (Methodist generally).

Many of them are well to do in the world and on
Sundays dress like Broadway exquisites. As to
antislavery sentiments, as far as I could see or
hear, it seemed to amount to this, that slavery
was a great inconvenience and trouble to the
whites and hurtful to the outward prosperity of
the State. " They disliked it as much as anybody could ; but there it was, without their fault,
and they did n't see how they could get rid of
it, but supposed by and by it would disappear.
They would not have the slaves set free to
remain among them, idle and vicious as they
were ; the North might take them, since it had
such a fondness for them ; at any rate, if we were
sincere in our desire to set them free, we had
better put our hands into our pockets and remu-
nerate their masters, etc., etc." This was the
amount of what I could gather amid the many
inconsistent and contradictory views of those
with whom I talked about it. The main difficulty
is that the *moral* idea is scarcely thought of.
Nobody feels that it is wrong, but only an inconvenience and economically a bad system. It may
be the business of the Northern abolitionists to
give them this moral idea, though they have
been slow to take it, and never may. While I
was coming on, I was much "exercised" as to
whether I should or should not preach about the

matter.   Feeling sick and nervous and unable to write, I doubted whether I could say anything worth while ; then came up doubts of the purity of my motives ; whether I should n't be doing it from vanity, or a spirit of bravado ; then, whether my words would be wise and calm enough, physically out of order as I felt, and so on.   Then, two successive weeks, I had to attend funerals, and hated to meet the mourners with a reform sermon, and so it came to the last service, and I had said nothing directly about the matter. Then I said, It will never do; and I sat down before going into church and hastily wrote two pages about the war and two about slavery, such as they were, and went into church, taking the sermon called " Repent, the cry of the prophet," read "Cry aloud, spare not," etc., from Isaiah, and then preached.   What I said about slavery was very calm and not the least in the " spare not " vein, only urging that if they saw this thing to be an evil, as they profess, they ought not to be indifferent or to acquiesce in it ; nor to be content with deploring it ; but in earnest to do something, or begin to do something, to remove it.   That the way of duty was clear ; that God would give unexpected help in the way of right, and that the difficulties would vanish before faith and a sincere purpose.   That each should do what he could, — feel, speak, plan, or execute as God had given power. This was what I said, encouraging rather than denouncing, and all brief and hasty. Sam, they took it beautifully ; nobody *went out*, and some stopped to say good-by to me at the door.

The next day I did not learn that anybody was offended except some *Northern* people. Mr. Abbott said, Sunday evening, that he had always told the people that there was little use in having a pulpit unless it was to be free on this as on all subjects. Still, I doubt whether they would settle a known abolitionist.

I am here in Philadelphia spending a rainy Sunday. I stayed to hear Furness. It was rather too intellectual a sermon, but he said some excellent things. . . . Think of these horrid people illuminating, as they did here and in Baltimore and Washington, for the Mexican barbarities ! I felt more indignant about that than about slavery. And these miserable Whigs now taking advantage of Taylor's corrupt popularity to ride into power, after all they have said about the war ! Dr. Dewey preached a fine sermon at Washington about political morality, which was good enough to give offense to the politicians.

TO SAMUEL JOHNSON.

BRATTLEBORO', May 20, 1847.

DEAR SAM, — I am having a very pleasant time here ; but between walking and watering have little leisure to write. . . . Having been waked, nearly an hour before, by the tramping of people past my door to their baths, I am invaded by a German Heinrich, who takes my bathing-sheet, and swathing myself in a blanket like an Indian chief, I follow him into the bathroom, where I sit down in a long tub and have water poured over me, and am rubbed for a time ; then dried on said sheet, bandaged, and dismissed to dress and walk half or three quarters of an hour before breakfast, generally taking the " circle," as it is called, across the brook and round by the D.'s, where I stop under the trees and drink a couple of tumblers of water. After breakfast, walking again, rambling, exploring, stopping, alone or in company. Sam, there are the love-liest places you ever saw, to search after and enjoy ; ravines, hills, wood-paths, cascades, green meadows. So till eleven o'clock, when I again resort to the bathroom and sit down in a tub of cold water, clothed in the aforesaid blanket ; and when we get a number together along the sides of the room, it is wonderfully suggestive of an

Indian council or pow-wow. Bandages renewed, and then a walk again to "get up a reaction," that is, to prevent being chilly. This brings me to dinner with a ravenous appetite. After dinner, lounging, talking, music, battledore for a while, or reading and writing, perhaps a siesta till four or five ; then, after another sitz-bath, a walk of an hour till tea. After tea, walk, stroll, read newspapers, play, sing; perhaps there is dancing in the saloon, or other family amusements. . . . So much for my life here. I write with my body swathed in moist linen bandages, which impart a constant, not disagreeable sense of coolness and moisture.

Of Furness and the Dudleian lecture, — what a pity you should n't have been there! Well, you shall read it. He said we must not look out of Christianity for natural religion, but into it. It was the *only* natural religion, what man was made for and must come to. Christ was not apart from Nature, but a part of Nature, his miracles and all. The common view of miracles was low and narrow, he said. There were some very eloquent episodes ; one about childhood. One or two *strong* sentences about the war and slavery ; too short for anybody to go out, even a law-student. The only difficulty, I thought, was that the idea, a new one to many, though old to

Furness (and you and me), was not brought out with quite sufficient distinctness, especially for those who were not familiar with Furness's writings. The fact is, it was the very ground taken in Parker's sermon, so far forth as this, that Christ did not create the truths he uttered, but saw and stated eternal truths; which seems obvious enough, but is not commonly recognized. Some people were enthusiastic; others praised cautiously; others thought it novel and rather dangerous, — and so, I fear, he is too much of a heretic for the Hollis Professorship.

TO SAMUEL JOHNSON.

BRATTLEBORO', June 12, 1847.

DEAR SAM, — Here are some hymns I got from the "Christian Lyre." These Methodist and Baptist people's "second coming" hymns make grand reform ones. But how meagre their idea of the meaning is; a personal salvation, while the world (which Christ came to save) all goes to red-hot destruction. But the churches are waking up, Sam, all about. The "New England Conference" (I don't know of what sect it is) has passed some strong resolutions and statements against slavery, and the Methodists of Accomack County, Virginia, came out so strongly, not long since, that a public indignation meeting was called to see that the republic received no detriment. The leaven is at work. Charles Sumner has sent me his "White Slavery in the Barbary States," interesting historically and a sort of covert *argumentum ad hominem*, all along, to our slaveholders and slavery-excusers. The parallel is ingeniously suggested and sometimes applied. All helps, plain words and parables. But, Sam, no peace yet! Well, we will be patient, — be "partners of Christ's patience." Is n't that a fine phrase? . . .

As to ——, Sam, I don't know; we will talk about it.

> "Where love is absent, works are found
> As tinkling brass, an empty sound."

I do *not love* them. If it were marriage, that would be enough. (I am now entirely versed in all the mysteries and responsibilities of love and matrimony, having just finished Harriet Martineau's love-novel "Deerbrook.") I am enjoying myself very much, but do not feel much effect from the waters yet. Sam, not one of the baths is so violent or disagreeable as a blister, the commonest resort of allopathy. Our life is easy and social, quite like a Phalanstery, I sometimes think; stated baths being substituted in place of labors.

So, Sam, you must come. I long for you not exactly in a thirsty land, but in a beautiful one, flowing with milk and water, spiritually thirsty, perhaps. But " I live in the outward now ; " I am only sorry that I don't feel myself getting well, stronger, and less nervous.

TO SAMUEL JOHNSON.

BRATTLEBORO' BATHING-TUB, July 5, 1847.

DEAR SAM, — . . . You see I am still among the mountains and the springs. Not finding so speedy benefit as I had hoped, and not finding so hot weather as I feared, I have concluded to stay a little longer. . . . The first of August I mean to go to Portland. And, Sam, I must have a visit from you there. . . . And there, in the old house and in the little upper room, scene of many boyish dreams and hopes and conflicts and visions, we will put in order the new hymn-book [second edition]. . . .

I was in MacIntire's pulpit yesterday, and it being Fourth of July, could not but give them a page or two on the war and slavery. They will be quite ready for you! . . . Your words give me strength.

TO SAMUEL JOHNSON.

PORTLAND, August 7, 1847.

DEAR SAM, — You see I have bidden adieu to Bathing-Tubs, mountains, and springs, and descended to the level of the sea. It has rained ever since I have been here, almost, and so, cut off from my baths and my walks at once, I don't feel quite so well for the change ; but I shall get into the sea as soon as practicable. . . .

I preached at Brattleboro', Sunday, on the Sufferings of Christ. In the afternoon, William Channing on Patience. It was a beautiful sermon, not quite so *eloquent* as I expected. The theme and occasion were not such as to rouse him, I suppose. He wove it upon my morning's sermon, beginning, "Our thoughts were this morning turned to the consideration of the sufferings of Christ. He was presented to us as a man. There are two other views held by Christians ; one which regards him as the Incarnate God, and one which considers him as a mediator. But looking at the sufferings of the man, what is so beautifully conspicuous through all as his patience," and so on.

So you see, Sam, mine is a "humanitarian" sermon everywhere. Channing is not satisfied with this view, with the view presented in Furness's Dudleian.   Regarding not so much the individual but the *race*, — the *man*, or Humanity, — he says this aggregate man must have some Head, and Christ is this.   That is not very clear to me, as I told him ; when he went on to say that as in progressive series we see first inanimate nature, then living things, then man, always rising upward towards God ; there must, at last, be some link in the chain which will come next to God, and directly communicate life from Him to, and so through, the rest to the lowermost. Christ is this link ; in other words, he is the Mediator.   Many things suggested themselves after this statement, but I had not a chance to talk with him farther.   He shocked some people by introducing and dwelling upon the idea that God *suffers* with men ; that He could not be the Father if He did not ; if He did not feel pain in view of all this evil and suffering.   But, Sam, I think of Him as seeing, *through* all, the great Light and Glory, seeing all the clouds float into light.   I cannot receive that idea, at least in the common meaning of *suffering*.   But how language fails in trying to speak of God !

TO SAMUEL JOHNSON.

PORTLAND, September 11, 1847.

DEAR SAM, — . . . I have lingered here longer than I meant to ; but now, resisting all enticement of cheap boats and sleepless, poisonous nights on board, I shall take the cars Wednesday morning, and on reaching Newburyport shall go at once to the church to help ordain Wentworth [Higginson]. Dr. Nichols goes with some reluctance, not approving of no-council innovations. Said he would n't go but for Wentworth, or some other particular friend, thus leaving a corner open for me, you see. He has never said a word to me about your sermons. L. thinks he was a little frightened, and that his next sermon was meant as an antidote. There is much talk about you, though ; several much delighted and interested. One lady asked me if you were a *Deist*, seeing you did n't speak of Christ through the whole service ! Strange that Deist, i. e., *Godist*, should be thought a bad thing or name! I, however, enlightened her. I have worked over those hymn - book manuscripts, copying hymns, etc., almost every day. . . . I have made some beautiful chants from the Apocrypha, *Deistic* wretch that I am ! I have found in a paper a good temperance hymn.

After his stay at the water cure, Mr. Long-fellow resumed candidating. One of the places he visited, a beautiful rural city of central New England, in which dwelt a peculiarly refined and cultivated society, attracted him greatly, and it was, perhaps, a real loss to both the people and the minister that (as Colonel Higginson writes) "The parish was tardy, and their invitation did not come until after he had accepted a call to Fall River. He wrote to me, with real feeling, about it, and said, 'If ever a man felt drawn to a place, that man was I, and that place was ———.' Then he admitted the comparative barrenness of Fall River (at that time a new manufacturing town), and ended, 'But Mount Hope shines fair in the distance, and I am content.' This was a type of his life; for him, Mount Hope always shone in the distance, as fair as the actual mountain from Fall River."

VI

FALL RIVER

Mr. Longfellow's first pastorate was assumed
under a genuine impression of duty. Perhaps it
is not always best that inscrutable personal lean-
ings should be rigidly controlled.

TO EDWARD EVERETT HALE.

CAMBRIDGE, November 21, 1847.

Dear Edward, — . . . I have just had a conversation with Ephraim Peabody [then Rector
of King's Chapel], a sort of " charge " from him,
which I like much better thus in private than in
the usual public way. He has inspired me to
take some great plans or ideas into my head, and
sacrificing romance and hopes of sympathy and
of the enjoyments of cultivated social intercourse,
to go straight to Fall River and make the church
over, or build up its growth after my own ideas.
. . . My own impression of the place has been
that, as a new, busy, and growing one, it was a
good place for action and influence ; that a man
must go there willing to depend upon himself for

impulse, except so far as he should find it from distinctly seeing the needs of the people, and desiring to meet them. The town is beautifully situated, but new and crude, in itself offering little to gratify the æsthetic taste ; the people, occupied in "business," having little time for social intercourse or culture, but kindly and ready to be influenced. A place, as yet, not crystallized ; increasing by a thousand or so a year in population, where a man of sufficient force might impress himself as far as he chose, and give his own "color to the alum-basket." All this attracts me, and I am on the point of writing a letter of acceptance ; when up rises a vision of forlornness and barrenness, and I pause.

This conversation with Peabody has done more than any one thing to make me say I will go, turning my back on doubts, but whether an hour hence will not find them fully alive, I know not. The people seem liberally disposed. The spokesman of the committee, an intelligent man, and of influence there, writes me that they won't care a fig about having an ordaining council ; . . . of his own accord he proposed to me that I should suggest to the Society that I should preach but *one sermon* a week, having a devotional service or Sunday-school on the other half-day.

TO SAMUEL JOHNSON.

FALL RIVER, November 29, 1847.

DEAR SAM, — Behold me here! Not yet settled, but in imminent peril of being. The week before Thanksgiving, a gentleman wrote to me that I was sent for from Fall River, and for three Sundays; I told him I would go for two, but would n't engage farther; so I came down here on the 20th, and spent a dark, lowering Sunday, thinking Fall River the most dismal place, almost, I was ever in. Monday morning I was off at daylight, and on Saturday came again. The sun shone out a little, and things looked altogether more attractive. The committee had begged me to come prepared to spend the week. . . . I am astonished to find that I can look with any complacency upon the place, so forlorn did it seem to me at first, including the church, which John Ware thinks so beautiful, and which I dislike as much. Well, last night, I being at tea with one of the congregation, Mr. B. entered and informed me that at the meeting of the Society after church services, a strong desire had been manifested to give me a call! I was taken by surprise. I told him that my wish had been not to be settled till the spring, though I wanted to preach during the winter. He said that they wished to ascertain whether I was in a condition to accept a call, and that a committee would confer with me, etc. . . . A week ago, I should have been ready to say, "No," at once; now I am surprised at myself that I do not say it, — but I do not.

Sam, there are many new societies springing up which one would like to look at first. They look upon this as a new society, however. It certainly needs building up from the present handful. Am I the man, and is this my place? I am inclined to think I ought to be in a town, — but why need I trouble you with my pro's and con's? Perhaps you do not know . . . how much such a matter as this harasses me. . . .

Sam, I believe it is the bay which has charmed me; I know not what else!

TO SAMUEL JOHNSON.

Boston, December 11, 1847.

DEAR SAM, — . . . Of Fall River. I have more than half a mind to go there. I see that I must lay aside all æsthetic and romantic dreams, the ideal church and other ideals, for a long while at least, if I go. Must give up things that I am right in valuing. . . . On the other hand, I see it is a centre of influence; it is not yet crystallized, is free to be moulded. I think I could do there as

I wish, so soon as they have become acquainted with me. I saw some kind-hearted men and women. Last Sunday morning I preached my "Coming to Christ." I threw in an extempore paragraph on the absurdity of denying the Christian name to men who did n't believe the miracles, that they might understand my theological position. B. walked home with me; liked the sermon very much. Yesterday came a note from him saying that, being very desirous of pursuing the study of Christ's life, he had determined, if I should come to Fall River, to devote five hundred dollars, in the course of three or five years, to the purchase of books under my direction that might help in the investigation. Now, I must say that one man so interested as that would be worth much to any minister.

At the hotel, I saw several young men (and there must be plenty in the town) whom I thought I could bring into my church. I was sorry that I could not see more of the people; but, as I said, they did n't come near me. Busy all day and tired at night, I suppose. . . . The most interesting thing I saw was an evening school (free) for young men over sixteen, working-men, you know, boys from the country and the like.

TO SAMUEL JOHNSON.

CAMBRIDGE, December, 1847.

DEAR SAM, — . . . The die is cast, the cup taken! Saturday I sent my letter of acceptance to Fall River, resisting the allurements of an invitation to preach in the Church of the Messiah, New York, and an appealing letter from Albany. I wrote two letters, . . . one to the committee containing business matters, — such as the congregational ordination; one sermon a week; new hymn-book; vacation. And the other to the Society, to be read after the first should be satisfactorily arranged, containing matters of sentiment, anti-sectism, freedom of speech, reform, etc. I hope that I may have a hymn from you for the ordination, and shall keep a place open.

TO EDWARD EVERETT HALE.

PORTLAND, January 31, 1848.

DEAR EDWARD, — I ought not to have let the newspapers be the first to tell you of my wedding-day with the bride, the church of Fall River. . . . There is to be no council. I am disappointed that Dr. Nichols will not be present to lay his hand upon my head and give his paternal blessing; but he hates to leave home, especially in winter, and, I doubt not, has a lurking objection to taking part in such *unconciliatory* measures as I have suggested. So I have asked Ephraim Peabody, who is apostolical and friendly, and indifferent to councils, and for whom I preached the other day in Boston.

The ordination and installation took place upon the 16th of February, 1848. Charles H. Brigham, of Taunton, offered the introductory prayer. John Weiss, of New Bedford, preached a powerful and striking sermon, on "The Modern Pulpit." Dr. Convers Francis, of the Divinity School, offered the ordaining prayer and gave the charge; George Ware Briggs, a former pastor, then of Plymouth, delivered the address to the people, and John F. W. Ware, more recently pastor of the Society, extended to his successor the right hand of fellowship. Edward Everett Hale read from the Scriptures. The first hymn sung was by the new pastor, and Henry W. Longfellow wrote for his brother that altogether perfect one, beginning

> " Christ to the young man said : ' Yet one thing more,
>   If thou wouldst perfect be.' "

Of the service, and its effect upon his own feelings, Mr. Longfellow wrote to Mr. Johnson, " I rejoice that the ordination services so much impressed you. The only want I felt was of something more of a devotional tone to meet *my own* feelings at the time. The prayer was almost the least moving thing to me, of all ; but during the whole of it, that line of Henry Ware's hymn ran in my mind, 'Sin, sloth, and self abjured before the altar,' which, indeed, contains all that could be said. The 'right hand' was the most interesting part to me. I could not give to the sermon the close attention it needed, but I felt it was an admirable statement of what so much needed to be said distinctly now."

The exercises were printed, and he says to Hale, " I write this note that I may put it into the post, together with a copy of the sermon, which please accept with all those friendly regards which I dared not put upon its front. If, from a pure love of the place of your adoption, you get your ordination sermon printed at a provincial press, you subject yourself to some delay, and get a provincial-looking pamphlet, after all. Still, *civitatis regimine donatus* though you are, I trust you will look with complacency upon these somewhat dim pages, and let some memories of the occasion shine through them. Weiss has added a page or two, to give more completeness to his statement. He loses something in the reading. His face, and the quaintness of his voice and manner, so precisely fitted to his style, and so entirely the complement of his words, are wanting. Yet they are readily summoned by one who heard them."

Samuel Longfellow had now fully entered upon real life. He had matured slowly, but was coming into full possession of his powers and understanding of himself. He was twenty-nine years of age; thoroughly educated, both generally and professionally; of rare personal culture and delicàte traits of mind, which adorned without weakening the firm moral substance of his manhood. "He was a difficult person to delineate," writes Colonel Higginson, "from the very simplicity and perfect poise of his character. He was, in the old phrase, 'a very perfit gentil knight.' He had no exceptional or salient points, but an evenness of disposition which, from boyhood onward, kept him not only from the lower temptations, but the higher ones. This was true of him when I knew him in college, and true at every later period. One could not, for a moment, imagine him vexed, or petty, or ungenerous. Few men have led a life of such unbroken calm and cheerfulness. At the same time, he was equal, in strength of character, to any emergency, and would have borne himself firmly upon the rack when more boisterous men failed. . . . He went about your room, as a lady once said, ' murmuring little charities ; ' for every book, every picture, he had a word of kindly apology, making the best of it ; but he had his own standard of right, and adhered to it with utter fearlessness. He did not strive, nor cry, nor did any man hear his voice in the streets ; but on any question requiring courage, he held the courageous side."

Another classmate in the Divinity School [1] writes of him, as he knew him at that period : " He was singularly quiet and undemonstrative. He made no professions of friendship, no display of knowledge, never argued or dwelt on differences of opinion, uttered no uncharitable imputations. Himself the soul of sincerity and truth-loving, he seemed to assume that all were similarly disposed. At first, he appeared to me utterly oblivious of the darker sides of human character, as if he did not recognize that there was any such thing as sin in the world, or any occasion for a struggle against evil in our own souls. This, I found afterwards, was my own mistake. It came from his disposition always to look upon the bright side, both in his estimate of others and in his own experience. By his clear, optimistic faith, he discerned, beyond the struggle, the final victory and peace. I felt

[1] The Rev. Ephraim Nute.

deeply his superiority of character, his Christ-like spirit. Among the advantages of the school, I esteemed his influence one of the richest. There was a nameless calm, a gentleness mingled with earnestness and strength, a fine poetic spirit. He filled a large place in my remembrance as one to whom I owe much which yet I cannot clearly define."

As he began his Fall River pastorate, Mr. Longfellow's health was still unsatisfactory, although improved by the rest he had enjoyed during the previous summer. He was consciously accepting a difficult post of service, but one to which he felt generously challenged.

In his opinions he had reached substantially, although he had not yet fully explored it, the religious position which characterized him throughout coming years. While, up to this time, he retained much of the phraseology and peculiar sentiments of Christianity, he was already, like Theodore Parker (to use the term now gaining currency), a "Theist," in that, in his religious life, his devout sentiments and aspirations, he admitted no mediator between himself and the Divine Spirit. He conducted his religious work under the spiritual leadership of Jesus, crediting his miracles and resurrection, and recognizing in him qualities highly excep-

tional. Yet he interpreted the endowments of
Jesus in accordance with a strictly humanitarian view, on the naturalistic principles which
Furness was now urging with so much force and
attractiveness. He was poetical rather than
mystical in temperament ; an intuitionalist in his
philosophy ; a transcendentalist in his thought
of the relation of man to God, to himself, and to
the facts of being.

But the ethical element was always the deepest of all in Samuel Longfellow, and was becom-
ing prominent in his thought, his preaching, and
his views of professional duty. To the reforms
of the day, especially the antislavery reform, he
was giving an ardent sympathy and increasing
attention. The "funnier things yet" which, a
few years before, he had expected to see, were
now the grave subjects of his most earnest
thought and sense of duty. In political affairs,
at this time so agitated and ominous, he took
the eager and serious interest of a patriot and a
moralist, hesitating never to refer to them, in
his mild but emphatic and persuasive way, in
his Sunday discourses.

As a parish minister, Mr. Longfellow's forte
was always in the close personal relations he
knew how to establish between himself and his
people. As he had foretold, his power in the

pulpit lay in reaching individual hearts with truth, more than dealing with abstruse and difficult questions of philosophy and theology. Or, rather, the former was the aim he peculiarly cherished in all parts of his ministry. He had a singular gift of " understanding " others, their trials, perplexities, and cares, their moral struggles and spiritual wants; and the art of helping and cheering them by kindly, wise suggestions and delicate attentions. Both men and women were drawn to him by a power of which they could hardly explain the charm. For children he had always an especial love and care, and won their affections as he did those of their elders. Their love for him was instinctive; they trusted him, and clustered about him, by a natural impulse which it scarcely required words for him to excite. His gentle manners, grave but genial, his pleasant humor, the quickness of his sympathies on all sides, the transparency of his religious emotions and moral instincts, the quiet wisdom of his practical thought, won the confidence of growing youth, of the sorrowing, the doubting, the troubled in mind, and prepared them to accept inspiration, guidance, or comfort. The absolute truthfulness of his character took from all his ministrations among his people the professional air, and made them the affectionate expres-

sions of trusty friendship. Old observances became instinct with fresh reality and significance.
He could not be restricted in his sympathies or
services to the limits of his parish, but, much
more a man and citizen than a minister, he over-
flowed in good works to all about him whom in
any way he could reach.

The obstacles to his full success in his chosen
calling were poor health, and a sensitiveness of
which it was partly the cause, and which was
doubtless excessive. The former impaired his
energy ; the latter caused him to undervalue the
services he rendered to those about him. His
instinct of spontaneity made formality impossible
to him, and custom irksome. A growing individualism, which he shared with Weiss, Frothingham, Higginson, and others of the brightest minds
of the day, was weakening his sympathy with the
majority of the Unitarians and the organized
work of the body. A highly æsthetic temperament created wants which were imperious, but,
in the prosaic life of New England fifty years
ago, not easily satisfied. His conscience often
reproved what was wholly constitutional and a
necessity of his being.

Few situations are less inspiring than that of
a clergyman settled in a small community given
up to material interests ; over a church feeble

in numbers and spiritual life, in which the attention of the members who really care for its welfare is absorbed in filling the seats and collecting ever-insufficient dues. In such a position a man needs not only fervor of purpose, but a deep insight and much practical wisdom, to discern his opportunity and its rewards.

Mr. Longfellow began his work at Fall River, as was intimated above, in a spirit of earnestness which was better than enthusiasm, and with as clear a comprehension as was perhaps possible, to a neophyte, of its difficult conditions. But when the excitement of installation in his new post had subsided ; before he had formed organic relations with the life of the community, or had become acquainted with his people ; condemned to live at a wretched country hotel, to eat his solitary meals in a bustling dining-room ; scarcely meeting his parishioners except at church, and expected to produce two discourses each week, our young minister, at first, found the situation dreary. He discovered a few congenial women ; among men, the only one who supplied to him that near companionship which was so needful to him was a " transcendental music-teacher, who has some good ideas and a deep, true feeling for his art." The poverty of suggestion in his conditions, out of which sermons could not flow and could with difficulty be squeezed, his conscientious mind too willingly interpreted as "spiritual deadness" in himself. He needed philanthropic activities, the sphere of which he could not immediately find amid a prosperous, self-sufficient, busy population. To the prescriptive duties of his post he gave himself faithfully, already characteristically trying to make all religious occasions genuine and freshly significant. His first communion-service was an occasion of much moment to him. He wrote to his friend Hale for suggestions as to its mode, and reported its celebration both to him and to Johnson, and especially in a thoughtful, affectionate letter to his mother, whose heart would naturally be deeply with her son on an occasion which, in those days, was felt to be of so much importance and significance.

TO EDWARD EVERETT HALE.

FALL RIVER, March 1, 1848.

DEAR EDWARD, — On next Sunday is my first communion. My wish is to have it open to all, and if possible to have the whole congregation remain, even if they do not all partake of the bread and wine. I think this is your plan. Will you tell me how you arranged it, whether you sent the bread and wine to all, or whether you asked those who wished to partake to come up to the table and receive them? I like the last plan the best, if the people will not feel shy about it.

. . . I, the solitary, am not yet "set in a family." For the time, it is more convenient, if not so pleasant, for me to remain here at the hotel. I hope by and by to find some pleasant house where I can have a sight of the bay. There is as lovely a water-view as you will easily find, short of the actual ocean. Failing of this, I think I shall fall back on my pastoral right to a home in the parsonage, which has passed into the hands of a member of the society. It is in a quiet shady nook and very inviting, save in being cut off from the sight of the water.

I am not exactly the solitary, though of course companionless. Three little families of my flock live in this house, and among them at least one intelligent and sympathetic woman. The people are not very demonstrative, or *vocative*. It strikes one oddly to find that nobody seems to have been here above a few years. You ask some questions about the place and are answered, "Oh! I came here only six months ago," or, "We moved here last year," or, "When we came here, some three or five years since," and so on. There are no aborigines, evidently, since the skeleton in armor was burnt. And they all unite in abusing the place and saying how unsocial it is, whereas if all these agreeable people would but come together once or twice a week they might have the pleasantest society. The town, under this spring sun, appears to me altogether fairer than when I saw it in December. I find too, already, more of cultivation than I expected, at least among the women. It is harder for me to get at the men, who are never at home. I have been in very good spirits, bating some dyspepsia. Before long we must explore the shortest road between Worcester and here. . . . Write as soon as you can and often — to the Bishop of Fall River,   SAM'L ✠ F. R.

TO HIS MOTHER.

MOUNT HOPE, March 7, 1848.

MY DEAR MOTHER, — I think you will be interested to hear of my first communion; so I shall delay my pastoral visits this afternoon till I have written you a brief account of Sunday's service.

I learned that the number of communicants was small, though the invitation had been always extended to all. The service was appointed for the afternoon, as there is always the largest attendance in that part of the day. In the morning I preached a sermon, giving my views upon the communion; that it was one of the ministrations of religion which should be open to all with entire freedom; and that all should *feel* at liberty to unite in it; that it should be a simple, cheerful commemoration of Christ, from which all feeling of dread should be banished; that no one need shrink from coming to the table of him whose love was toward all men, and who ate with publicans and sinners, any more than he need shrink from approaching in prayer the All Holy Father. I dwelt somewhat upon these points, endeavoring to remove the unfounded and injurious feeling of awe and mystery which, to many minds, veils this rite, and I closed by saying that I should invite *all* to unite with us, who should feel at the time a desire to do so, whether they had ever before or not, and whether they would ever again or not; that some might find satisfaction in partaking of the bread and wine, and others be best helped by joining in spirit in the prayers, the meditations, the associations of the time. I wished first and most of all to impress a sense of *perfect freedom;* thinking this essential to open the way to a spiritual understanding and reception of the rite. In the afternoon, the whole service — hymns, scripture, and prayer — was made a remembrance of Jesus. I preached my. sermon on the sufferings of Christ, closing it with a reference to the communion and a repetition of my desire that all should feel at liberty and welcome to unite with us. Then I gave a benediction, and after a pause of a few minutes, that any might have an opportunity to retire who wished, I came down to the table. Not a person left the house. I made a short extempore address, applying more particularly the sentiment of the sermon, and then a prayer. Then, breaking the bread, with the usual words, I took it from the table and carried it myself to each pew, offering it to all, and the same with the wine, repeating at intervals appropriate sentences from the Scriptures. Only a few partook of the elements, perhaps none who had not been accustomed to do so. We then united in a silent prayer, followed by the Lord's Prayer and the benediction.

The only thing that was not entirely pleasant to me was the feeling that those who did not partake of the elements might feel an embarrassment at refusing what yet they did not feel quite prepared to receive, and it would have been pleasanter, certainly to me, if all or nearly all had partaken of the bread and wine. I think that if they continue to remain, more and more will gradually do so.

I liked very much the distributing the elements myself rather than by deacons ; it is simpler and less sacerdotal and official.   It brought me nearer to my people.   It seems, too, to be carrying out the spirit of the chapter which I had read, where Jesus washes his disciples' feet, and says that he came not to be ministered unto but to minister. It was suggested to me by Mr. Ware.   I felt the more encouraged to hope that all would remain, from Edward Hale's having told me that they did so from the first in his church.   I have been glad to find from several who have since spoken to me that the service was generally felt to be very interesting.   I suspect the only way to induce all the congregation to remain is to make the communion a part of the service of the day, and not a separate service, as is usual.

It is some time since I heard from home.   I am well, except some dyspeptic symptoms, and very contented and comfortable.   I have called upon about half the families of the parish, but I have to go alone, and I find only the women at home, — the husbands being at the shops, day and evening; but I see some of them there. Almost every house holds two families, one up-stairs and one below, a mode of division which is a peculiarity of the place, I think.   But if the house is square, it is made to accommodate three or four families.   Rather too compact stowage, I think, but the families are mostly small.

Notwithstanding the importance which the young minister seemed, naturally, to attach to the celebration of the communion, we can discern in the last letter that his deepest interest was, really, in giving new life, and especially the spirit of freedom, to the ancient rite. And a scruple, which with his maturing thought ultimately became controlling, significantly makes its appearance in a letter which, soon after this, he wrote to Mr. Johnson. "I begin," he says, "to have something of Higginson's feeling about the word 'Christian.'" On the same date, another brief paragraph reveals characteristic tendencies of thought and feeling. "Is it not inspiring to see those French idealists so swaying the people? Here it is thought that only the lowest motives and most material considerations are to be addressed to them, — that they cannot appreciate anything higher. The faith of these men is beautiful. Sam, this thing cannot fail."

TO SAMUEL JOHNSON.

FALL RIVER, June 29, 1848.

DEAR SAM, — I have just come from Mount Hope. For months it has been beckoning to me across the water. Nay, it has been a friend of many years. On the walls of the chamber where I slept when a boy hung, and hangs still, a little

sketch in india ink of Mount Hope and the bay.
Was it destiny, prophecy? . . . The Hutchin-
son family came here to sing, and some of their
friends got up an excursion for them and asked
me to join them. Accordingly, at seven this
morning, we set sail under a shaded sky, and beat
over to the opposite shore, some six miles. . . .
The brothers are good-hearted and cordial, and
call you "brother" in a very pleasant way.
Mount Hope quite answered all my expectations,
and I at once entered into negotiations with the
woman at the red house at the bottom of the hill
to take me some day to board. We all drank at
the spring where King Philip quenched his thirst.
It is at the foot of a granite cliff, clambered all
over with grapevine and wild roses, in which is a
little recess called King Philip's seat. Here he
may very likely have sat, nourishing in his great
wild heart his schemes of resistance to the growing power of the whites. We climbed to the
top of the hill, and had a fine panorama of the
bay, . . . and the beautiful farm fields all lying
in the lights and shadows of a clouded sky. Then
we came down to the shadow of the old gnarled
apple-trees where our table was spread. The
skillful men and women concocted a chowder over
a gypsy fire, which we had just begun to eat
when down upon us came a tremendous shower,

which drove us and our baskets, well wetted, to the shelter of the red house. This only made us merrier, however. The Hutchinsons sang two or three songs, and then it was time to return. The wind had shifted, and we had to beat back again, but it was not tedious. The sun shone fair upon our town as we rounded the point, and on the wharf we bade good-by to our friendly singers. . . .

I am encouraged by the political disaffections in both parties, as showing that partisan bondage is loosing its hold. I hope little from political action against slavery. But so far as the government acts at all upon the matter, I wish it to be against rather than for slavery ; and if men opposed to slavery can conscientiously go to Congress, I am glad to have them there, and in the President's chair, too !

FALL RIVER, June —, 1848.

DEAR SAM, — At last we have the longed-for, the beautiful, hymn-book ! I am quite satisfied with its externals, — type and page are neat and agreeable. The supplement is grand, Sam, without a " stain of weakness ; " from beginning to end a fine, full strain of music, swelling, dying, varying in mood, but rising at last into a grand, triumphant swell of sure prophecy !

. . . I had a delightful visit at Newport; the fresh ocean air, the repose of the grass-grown streets, are delicious. It happened to be the day of the great Yearly Meeting of the Quakers. After our service I went into their vast meeting-house, but I got no seat, for the press, and so I soon came out, leaving a man lifelessly calling us through his nose to " go into the vineyard of the Lord." How I longed for somebody to speak a living word to that great concourse from a *real* "moving of the spirit." . . . The only chance I got to visit the beach was Sunday night in the moonlight, and then but for a moment; but I could not come away without seeing it. Newport is consecrated to me by the memory of Dr. Channing, and I feel each visit to be a pilgrimage. Have you read his Life? There are some beautiful incidents. But I fear it reveals too much the inward process of self - discipline. I shrink from reading such secrets, — they do not bear printing. Yet he [the editor] has kept back, with a true delicacy, the most interior expressions.

The confidential intercourse between Mr. Longfellow and Mr. Johnson discloses a perfect harmony, and the unrestricted but delicate intimacy of two rare and noble spirits. Letters, frequent and full, usually serious, often playful, always affectionate, passed between the pair. Whatever was of concern to either was eagerly discussed. Until a later date than the present, Johnson's do not come down to us, but their purport is to be inferred from those of his friend, which he more systematically preserved. Johnson was now passing through a trying period of candidature ; attracting by his intellectual power, his spiritual fervor, and his brilliant style, but alarming and offending by his frank avowals of theological heresies, and of antislavery and other reform sentiments. Longfellow wrote him again and again, wise, brave, and reassuring letters, well calculated to give him that encouragement of which, in his own despondent moments, he often betrayed his need to his "Damon," as he sometimes styled him. No experience was passed over unnoted, no emotion was unshared between these two friends. They found in each other something of that support and comfort which they were not seeking in the marriage state. Their joint enterprise, the hymn-book, had achieved the success of even a fourth edition, and the correspondence was still replete with suggestions about it, — and an occasional remittance. Among the concerns which presently engaged Mr. Longfellow, in his parish, was a very characteristic one. "I have been very busy, reading new books for the Sunday-school. Out of a hundred I rejected fully half, for bad sentiments." He also appealed to Hale, then editing a Sunday-school paper, for help. One phrase of the following letter shows that he had early instituted those intimacies with the children near him, which always made them at home wherever his own home was.

TO EDWARD EVERETT HALE.

FALL RIVER [no date].

DEAR EDWARD, — ... I have occasion to keep a store of little books for little children who come to my study, or to distribute in my Sunday school, and I am compelled for the most part to resort to the Sunday-school Union, which furnishes an abundant supply of such books of every size, very neatly printed and prettily illustrated. But those books are not safe ; they come in packages, and of every package several have to be burned ; others will do with pen-alteration of a word or two, and others again are very good. But I wish *we* could be as well furnished with books of the same style, built after our ways of thinking ; which would impress the lesson of truthfulness without allusions to the "lake of fire," and teach the presence of God in some other character than that of spy; and warn against evil without the exhibition of an angry God who holds "a rod to send young sinners swift to hell;" and tell of Jesus without stating the object of his life to be "to save us from going to hell;" and inculcate the importance of time without the stimulus of reference to the terror of death and the gloom of the grave.

Opening his heart to Johnson, he complains — the young minister's trial! — of dryness as to sermon-writing. "I did hope it would n't be so when I got into my own pulpit. But I don't yet feel identified with the people and somehow don't get *near* to them as I should like. But this must come in time, I suppose, following its own laws. ... "I visit daily a young girl, patiently sinking in consumption. Only now and then do I find what to say to her upon spiritual things. I find a prayer the best expression. I feel, Sam, that in visiting the sick, the minister should be able to carry with him an atmosphere of *physical health*, which would be as reviving as a breath of fresh air. Spiritually, I feel that he needs to reach that height which shall make him equally calm in the presence of the joyous and of the suffering; which shall practically reconcile those apparent contrasts and discords that are always side by

side in life, and from one to another of which he
may be constantly passing in his intercourse with
his people.   If he can look upon all as serenely as
God's light shines at once upon the festival and
the sick-chamber, the prison-cell and the work-
shop, then he will be welcome and helpful everywhere ; will be a true divine presence.   But what
self-conquest, and baptism of the spirit, before
that height of spiritual health can be reached ! "

About the same date : " I was sent for lately
to attend the funeral of a lady whom, or whose
family, I had never seen ; the body was buried in
a field near the house, and I made a prayer at the
grave [after the house service].   It was a country
funeral.   I liked the bearing of the coffin upon
the friendly shoulders to its private resting-place,
amid familiar scenes, so much better than the
long procession of carriages and an entombment
in a public graveyard.   Sunday, I attended the
funeral of the wife of one of my parishioners, of
whose sickness I had not even heard.   And on
Tuesday that of another parishioner, who died
suddenly, leaving a wife and young children.   It
is hard always to keep one's calmness and serene
faith amid so many tears, and at the same time
to sympathize with the sorrow.

. . . " You have heard of the death of John
Ware's wife.   He feels it deeply, but writes me

with calmness. He says, "All I do is in the thought of her, looking to a more precious ministry than ever before." Sam, this is a trial *we* cannot understand."

. . . "Last Sunday Charles Spear preached in my pulpit in the evening. I prepared the way for him by a morning sermon upon "Christ the judge of the world ;" speaking, first, of his judgment of individuals by the silent lesson of his character and life ; that pure, unfaltering tone which may show each of us how far we are from unison with God ; and secondly, of his judgment of man by the immutable laws of love to God and to man, which he proclaimed, and which are the standards by which all men and institutions are to be approved or condemned ; closing by an application of these laws to war, slavery, our present system of trade and labor, and our treatment of the criminal.

"I have been to the Kennebunk Ordination.[1] The services were good, but I was a good deal 'riled up' by the ministers ungenerously, as I thought, insisting upon calling themselves a *council*, which neither the minister nor the people desired. I even thought of writing to the 'Christian Register' about it, but afterwards cooled off, and saw that, whatever they called themselves,

---

[1] That of the Rev. Joshua Augustus Swan.

the *thing* did n't exist. . . . At the Boston station I found [Ralph Waldo] Emerson, going to Saco to lecture. It was a pleasant chance. He was very genial, and has much shrewd common sense. Rochester [spirit] knockings he could not away with (as indeed who can ?), and declared that 'Knockings were only for the Knockable.' *He* 'would n't hear them. If the good heaven comes down to earth, it shall at least be civil.' He told me of the people he met in England. Froude he liked very much. Francis Newman he did not like. Starr King appeared also, in the cars, go-ing — the way of all flesh nowadays — to lecture."

Presently our young pastor encounters another of the trials of the minister — the lay monitor. The issues of the time are intimated in the talk of his parishioner, the same good man who had offered such liberal assistance in studying the life of Jesus.

TO SAMUEL JOHNSON.

FALL RIVER, September 5, 1848.

DEAR SAM, — . . . I came back to Fall River on Thursday afternoon in the express train, which tore along without stopping and jarred my nerves in the most fearful manner. Thus wearied, I had hardly reached here when —— appeared and spent the whole evening, saying the

most disheartening things about the need of a
minister's recognizing the division of labor, and
confining himself to the elucidation of the gospel, leaving slavery and intemperance to be discussed by those who had had time and opportunity to examine these subjects thoroughly, —
as the minister could not if he attended to his
proper work. He said I was invited here, "not
to be a minister of religion, but a minister of
the gospel," etc. The answers were obvious,
but I was too weary to contend with him. It
chilled and discouraged me, though, to be met
thus on my return, and the next day I felt both
unwell and homesick, and did not write any sermon. Saturday, I wrote a Communion sermon;
the lesson of which was that the disciples needed
the remembrance not so much, not merely, for
their personal consolation, but because they had
a *work* to do, for which they must be strengthened by keeping alive their union with Jesus and
with each other, that each might feel that he
was strong by all this strength. So we, too,
have a *work* to do, since Christ's work was not
yet completed, nor God's kingdom come ; a work
indicated in his words, " Inasmuch as ye have
not done it unto one of the least of these my
brethren, naked, hungry, sick, in prison, ye have
not done it unto me ;" and I applied this espe-

cially to the call made upon a Christian church by the suffering and evil that existed in the narrow dirty streets and miserable houses where the Fall River poor live in want and sin. I have felt ever since I came here that I ought to do something for these children of wretchedness and neglect ; but have n't known how to get at them. Now, I have found one kind-hearted woman who visits them, and I mean to put myself under her guidance, and I hope soon to engage a little band of Christians in this work. I feel that a common object of this kind will do more than anything to bring about that union of interests of which there seems to be so little in my society.

Dear Sam, I have written a hymn for your ordination. I do not know how you will like it, for it is very general. What of Medford ? Shall I tell you what Stetson said to me in Boston, that their only doubt about asking you seemed to be in the feeling that you moved in too high a path of thought for the common people ? There are many, you know, who come to church to get a kind of comfort and cheer in their humble daily work, into whose sphere of thought and action great ideas do not enter. Now I believe you would meet these more, after you were settled and saw their need. But still, your work is rather that of a prophet, and seems to demand the moral wilderness of the city as its ground; where are thousands of active, restless minds needing to be set right rather than kept right, needing to be inspired rather than comforted. So, if you are not asked to Medford, think it is not the place for *you*. If you are, it will be the place for you, for a time certainly — am I right?

. . . Yesterday I got a letter from T.; after almost a year's silence; rather rhapsodical and pantheistic, but much in earnest. But, he says, "I must write to you in this tangent style, for I have been living with low-minded, jealous artists, and bodies of sweating models, and amid the low jokes and jargon of harlots; drawing from nude men and women, the human corruption from which art must spring, as the bird whose cradle is decay. In academies and schools, and amid the earthly tabernacles so polluted, one is in danger of forgetting the higher purposes of art. But now, away from all this (at the Baths of Lucca; were you there?), I can feel the old everlasting song sound within me, and I cannot resist the feeling which prompts me to give my better and constant nature wing." Why "*must* spring," Sam? Isn't it dreadful to know that it *does* thus spring? that our artists are thus trained? What can we expect of art, then? Yet it was so with Raphael. . . .

I see a notice in the street of the formation of a "Workingmen's Protective Union." I must inquire into it.

TO EDWARD EVERETT HALE.

FALL RIVER, January 9, 1849.

DEAR EDWARD, — I have been upon the hill to see the coasters, — the human *land*-coasters, I mean, — and their shouts still sound from afar. This excellent New Bedford idea has reached us this winter, and ladies and gentlemen renew their childhood and make sport of the downhill of life. I call it an excellent idea, and it surely is, to get people out of doors and engage them in exhilarating, healthful, and social amusement; better by far than being pent up in a ballroom. I don't see why coasting should n't become a national New England sport. . . . A man came to me lately to help him get work. I was not successful and it made me sad, feeling, moreover, that here was but one of so many. "A poor man seeking work and unable to find work; seeking leave to toil that he might be fed and clothed — and in vain; the saddest sight that fortune's inequality exhibits under the sun." In a world, too, where is so much work needing to be done. If we could but bring together the work and the man ready and anxious to do it! I feel a growing interest in these and other social questions, and no less strongly feel my inability to begin to fathom them, through want of knowledge. Pray communicate to me from time to time of yours, and indicate sources of information. Certainly one cannot look at the poverty, wretchedness, ignorance and inevitable sin which exist as a permanent element in our fairest communities, without a shudder at the terribleness of the evils of whose depth most of us have but faint conception ; and without feeling that it cannot be God's will that it should continue ; that it ought not by man's allowance and aid to continue. But — not to dwell in dreams of future and far off renovation — to discover what is to be done now, — *hic labor !* The evil is so vast, the problem so complicated, that appalled we ask where to begin, and he is a wise man who can answer. Plainly, the evil will not grow less or the problem clearer. Almsgiving, it is plain, is but superficial alleviation. Free education, doing so much, does not reach those most in need, — the lowest, and that an increasing class, — since of that the children are too useful at home to be spared for school. Our factories make the law a dead letter.

What do you know of Louis Napoleon ? He once wrote a book on pauperism, or some kindred subject, which shows a good tendency. His father was a man of beautiful character, which Goethe has finely delineated.

. . . A letter to-day from ——, who speaks of himself as disappointed in his efforts for a class of "workingmen" in Boston, and as feeling much alone in the world. But when I have met him, and felt anxious to give him my sympathy in his efforts and hopes, he has seemed so little to need it, to be so self-sustained and self-inclosed, that I have found myself unable. He seems to have taken on a "spherical" condition, and I cannot get into contact with him any more than the hot crucible with its drop of water. I should n't wonder if this were somehow the secret of his ill success in his educational efforts. He would fain help these less-favored ones, but he will not, or cannot, touch them. And I think his workingmen must feel as if there were a chasm between them and him, in spite of his sincere expressions of interest and his real desire to be of benefit to them.

I wish you would tell me of some of your practical plans and operations for the good of your church. I have little inventive faculty in this line.

TO SAMUEL JOHNSON.

FALL RIVER, February 27, 1849.

DEAR SAM, — . . . As to those men of —— you replied worthily. The fact is, being just launched, they were afraid you would upset their boat if they took you on board. But nothing can excuse their letter and its virtual prohibition of your fulfilling your engaged time. O men of much belief and little faith ! They wish to build up a Unitarian society, and dare not have a minister who will drive anybody away. They cannot spare men to go out of meeting ! You must go where a free church is to be built up on the basis of life ; which will choose a living minister before a comfortable one. Well, courage ! these wanderings of yours, preaching in the wilderness, are not in vain. Hearts and minds are stirred. It is not lifeless or vain preaching which brings such committee-letters. Only I hope your sermons are scrupulously *just*. I thought Wentworth's, strong, free, true as it was, *not* entirely just, since I doubt not there were many men who honestly thought (Heaven knows through what process of logic !) that a vote for Taylor was a vote for freedom. There was a vast deal of dust thrown into people's eyes.

Joshua Swan has lately preached for me. His

sermons gave me a great deal of pleasure, mainly
from their complete naturalness and simplicity.
They were upon quiet topics, charity, little sins;
full of the simplicity of a cultivated mind, and of
pure and gentle feeling. His nature is quiet, and
I was glad to see him true to it. Contact and
conflict will give him more fire. I long for the
power to clothe high and spiritual ideas in the
simplest, homelike language.

The 16th was the anniversary of my ordination. I gathered my people under my wing, in
the evening, in a social meeting at the parsonage. Some fifty came, and it was very pleasant
to me, and, I believe, to them. The Sunday
after, I preached a brief anniversary sermon to a
handful of people in a snowstorm. I could not
congratulate them upon an increase of numbers.
But I never had any extravagant hopes as to
numerical growth. I have neither the bustling
energy to bring people in, nor the popular ora-
tory to attract. I should be satisfied with our
numbers if there were more life. I know that
some are interested in my preaching, and do not
let myself doubt that it has done good, nor am
I discouraged. But I feel a lukewarmness and
passivity in the society which communicates
itself to me. At least, I have not spiritual life
enough to outweigh it. However, my temper-

ament indicates gradual operation to be my method, and I hope I am gaining power for more impressive action by and by.

With place and people personally, I am well content. But I do not find myself as yet taking deep root here. . . . Have I told you of my Friday evening meetings for the study of the New Testament? Our numbers have increased from two to half a dozen and sometimes nine! They are at my study, and are at times very interesting.

He early put his people to a simple moral test.

"The Universalist minister came to see me yesterday and I liked him; is from the West, having lived in Kentucky and Illinois. He has stentorian lungs — I heard him as I passed his church last Sunday. It will make my people stare to see him in our pulpit, but 't will do them good. And I shall not, like ——, ask them beforehand if they are willing to hear a Universalist, but take it for granted they have too much sense to object."

He habitually longs for the company of his friend; in almost every letter he calls for him : —

"The spring-magic touches even Fall River with beauty, and the houses that seemed so bare are veiled in clouds of rose color and white and

tender green. I am much abroad in the woods
and fields. When will you come and be my companion ? "

As he writes, on a Sunday afternoon, " A
preacher is holding forth in the hall across the
street, and his forlorn tones come through my
open windows. Oh! Sam, at times it comes
over one that all this preaching is terribly spec-
tral ! Only the remembrance of some heart-stir-
ring, living words, at intervals heard from pulpits
in times past, encourages us to hope that we too
may, at times, feed others with something more
than husks."

. . . " Last Sunday I was at home in the morning ; in the afternoon went to the Stone Bridge
[a mission station], and discoursed to quite a
numerous auditory, for an hour, upon man the
child of God, made in his image. 'Little lower
than the angels ' was my text ; and the greatness
and worth of the human soul, its divine capacities
and destiny, my theme. Needful words to them,
too seldom heard there before, I fear. To-day
they have a Baptist elder from Newport, and the
Sunday after I go again. It was beautiful, as I
stood in the pulpit, to look out through the windows or the open door upon the waters of the
bay, which come up within a short stone's throw
of the house.

. . . "I don't suppose I shall venture to write you or anybody from Niagara. If, as Emerson says, 'a great picture imposes silence' upon one, what must a great God-painting do?"

TO EDWARD EVERETT HALE.

OFFICE OF SCHOOL COMMITTEE,
FALL RIVER, May 9, 1849.

I write in an interval of official labors (!), with an official steel pen and official blue ink. . . . The exclamation point is not an ironical tone-mark, but an embodied sigh of weariness. Monday, yesterday, and to-day, I have been incessantly engaged, morning, afternoon, and evening, examining scholars and teachers, and a vista of work opens itself through the rest of the week which convinces me that I repose in no sinecure, for a time at least. . . .

TO SAMUEL JOHNSON.

FALL RIVER, May 17, 1849.

DEAR SAM, — I preached at Fair Haven Sunday, having been incessantly occupied the preceding week in the labors of school committee-man. In the cars I met Edward Hale, going to New Bedford. So Monday I brought him over here, and we spent a pleasant morning basking in the sunny fields.

Alcott wrote me a note of invitation to the
Town and Country Club. I thought your re-
marks on the club showed you slightly rabid.
Short of complete isolation, I can hardly imagine
anything that would less limit or label anybody
than paying five dollars for a share of a room
where you might meet the all-sided, motley, un-
labelable set of people who have got together in
this club, from Fields and Whipple to Garrison,
Parker, and Dwight. So don't bristle and put
out your quills (or your pen) against this harm-
less chimæra. . . . At the club meeting Hurlbut came out gallantly in favor of asking in the
women. Emerson and Dwight opposed, which I
should think quite un-Fourieritish. Wentworth
[Higginson] spoke also in favor of the fair. I
hear some talk of having Alcott to " converse "
here, if twelve " $\pi\nu\epsilon\upsilon\mu\alpha\tau\iota\kappa o\iota$ " can be found with
each two dollars in his or her purse.

Have you heard the Germania's exquisite music ? I am going over to New Bedford to-night
for the purpose. I heard them in Cambridge.

TO SAMUEL JOHNSON.

FALL RIVER, August 26, 1849.

DEAR SAM, — How beautiful the quiet of the
Sunday afternoon ! To sit and hear those soft-
clanging bells call the people to hot churches,

while I sit in a cool back room and wait till the shadows grow long before having to go out! I enlarge my phylacteries, and am to have this cool back room, which sees only the morning sun, besides my front parlor (no longer bed-ridden), where the afternoon rays are too fervent, and light must be shut out to keep away the heat.

. . . You have heard of my father's death, in the early morning of the day I reached home. It is a great comfort to me to have been with him [previously] in his sickness, to render those little attentions which are so great a satisfaction to our hearts. I felt nearer to him than I have ever done before. And we all had the strongest sense of his presence with us after he had left the body, a joyful presence, as of one from whom a cloud had passed and a burden fallen, and who now stood among us in health and new life, giving us his happy benediction. I am sure that sickness has often drawn a thicker veil between him and us while he dwelt in the flesh than death has now done, which seemed rather the lifting of a veil.

Mr. Longfellow's letter on the occasion of a brother's death, which took place a year later, is fittingly associated here with the last.

TO SAMUEL JOHNSON.

PORTLAND, September 17, 1850.

DEAR SAM, — I found that my brother had revived after they wrote me; but he was very sick, and is daily growing weaker. It seems impossible that he can continue more than a very few days. How strangely the vital powers resist the attacks of disease! Like the defenders of a besieged city, driven from outpost after outpost, rallying and retreating, till, shut up in the citadel, they stand at bay and hold out still. So powerful is life, so hard to conquer; anon, a slight obstruction, a pin's prick, and it is gone at once! Shall we ever so know and obey the physical laws that this bountiful energy shall have its full course? And then will there still be a limit, as we are wont to say, or will the thought of some prove true, that " death itself shall be abolished " ? Why may not the healthy process of renewal endlessly repair the daily and hourly waste? We say the soul would choose not to be confined forever in these fetters of the flesh, that its wings cannot expand here. But who has ever reached the possibilities of an earthly expansion? If, from year to year of man's physical prime, his mind enlarges in power and attainments, who can place the limit to this enlargement, suppos-

ing the body to be continually renewed ? Who
that dies oldest, most vigorous, having accomplished most of acquaintance with what this
world has to teach, has yet done more than begin
a knowledge of even the natural world ?

TO SAMUEL JOHNSON.

SACO, MAINE, October 22, 1849.

DEAR SAM, — Waiting here at Saco for the
cars, how can I better spend the rainy hour than
by resuming my intercourse with you ?

. . . I did not go to the convention, though I
wanted to hear Weiss's sermon on Inspiration. I
am glad he took that subject. I feel more and
more that the great doctrine that needs to be
preached into the ear of this generation is the
doctrine of the Holy Spirit, the word of the living, present God, which whoso receiveth, to them
it gives power to be the sons of God. This faith
only can redeem our age from materialism. This
alone can be — as it always has been, from Jesus
to George Fox and William Channing — the
life, the support, the strength of reformer, hero,
martyr, saint.

I was most forcibly struck, the other day, while
commenting upon the eighth chapter of John, to
see how this faith in the real presence lay at the
bottom of the soul of Jesus, coming to him now

as destiny: "He that sent me is with me;" —
now as consolation in loneliness, misunderstand-
ing, and misrepresentation: "I am not alone;"
— now as courage to proclaim the eternal and
divine truth, — he, an unknown, unlettered youth,
in face of the oldest and most reverend and
most learned: "I speak not from myself, I speak
the words of Him that sent me;" and so on.
Taking refuge constantly in this thought, driven
in upon it by outward opposition, and uttering
his most mystical sayings in answer to the cavils
of the dead-souled Pharisees, — not, it would
seem, for their enlightenment, but for his own
consolation and encouragement.

Sam, we must try to live in this faith. If God
be with us, we need not fear and cannot fail. If
we speak this word, which we have learned of
him, it cannot but be victorious, though we per-
ish. And how attain this faith? Jesus says:
"The Father hath not left me alone, because I
do always the things that please Him," "For I
came not to do my own will, but the will of
Him that sent me."

TO SAMUEL JOHNSON.

FALL RIVER, October 31, 1850.

... Think of our rising upon the city of Boston
in conjunction, the same Sunday! and — to drop

the astronomical figure — of my not knowing you were there. I had a good enough time at Chauncy Place. Do you know that the church is lighted by a ceiling of subdued glass? When this was put in, Arthur Gilman said it was the first time he had ever heard of trying to raise Christians under glass, adding that he now knew what was meant by "early Christians."

I tea-ed with Dr. Frothingham, who was kindly and social. O. B.'s mother told me how she tried to persuade him not to be a minister! — till one day he came to her and told her that he *must* be, when she ceased. . . .

Of Jenny Lind and the Fugitive Slave Law meetings, when we meet. I hope this golden weather will last your advent. But if tempests lower, we will have a cosy talk by the air-tight-stove-side.

TO SAMUEL JOHNSON.

FALL RIVER, December 3, 1850.

DEAR SAM, — Whence this silence? Ticknor told me he was about printing a new edition of a certain hymn-book, and I have sent him a long list of corrections. . . . Sam, of one grand thought I am sorry to find no expression in our book — God's pure justice, his eternal law of right. I suppose we could find no true expression of it,

most hymns so wretchedly pervert it. . . . Have
you read "Alton Locke"? It is charmingly fresh
and earnest. . . . It is said to be by a Church of
England minister. If so, he must be a very
liberal one. The theology is mainly very good,
with perhaps a little too much of what your
friend in Nantucket called "Jesusism." That I
do not understand, do not get hold of, wherever
I meet it. . . . This reminds me that —— called,
Sunday evening, and said he really had some
doubts whether he could conscientiously aid in
supporting preaching which he conscientiously
felt was so positively erroneous in its methods
and topics as that of our Unitarian pulpits,
though I don't think he finds anything elsewhere
that suits him better. . . . He is very sincere
about it, poor man, and always frank with me
and personally friendly, and I can't help feeling
that it is hard for him to sit under, and pay
largely for, what feeds him not and what he
thinks feeds not others, or feeds them amiss.
But what a dreadful state of spiritual dyspepsia
to get into, is n't it?

TO SAMUEL JOHNSON.

PORTLAND, March 17, 1851.

DEAR SAM, — I came down here last Thursday
on receiving a telegraphic note communicating

the sudden death of my mother ; sudden, but gentle and placid ; such a death as I have often heard her wish might be hers, and a fitting close to a life serene, quiet, loving, and holy.

I did not think I should ever weep again, at such a time ; but when I went at night to the chamber where, through my childhood, I slept next to my mother's, the remembrance of all the loving care which had embosomed those years came over me and forced tears that would not be stayed at once. Now I have only the most peaceful and happy thoughts, and sweetest sense of the presence through all the house of a meek and tranquil spirit, a spirit calm and gentle and full of love.

My mother had long been an invalid. I do not remember her as other than such. We had not supposed that she would stay here to number seventy-three years. But I know not how to be thankful enough for the guidance and influence of such a character and heart and life. She was remarkable for her piety, — the simplest, most unobtrusive, most childlike, most pervasive and controlling trust in God ; not very often spoken of in words, I think, but always speaking in the life ; in her daily patience, cheerfulness, calmness, and active goodness ; in the devout book she loved to have in her hand ; in her love for all things beautiful in nature, whether in commonest flower or the thunderstorm, which I first learned not to fear by seeing her always sit at the window to watch its glory.

She had remarkable calmness and self-possession, — the fruit, I believe, of her piety. It did not falter under many and frequent trials and sorrows. I shall not forget how, years ago, after the death of my almost twin sister, she stood with me beside the body and simply, by the cheerful calmness of her tones, took from me the dread of death. And severer trials than the death of children I have seen her bear with equal serenity.

Dear Sam, shall not such lives say to us forever, "Come up hither"? such guarding spirits keep us ever strong, holy, trustful, and untrembling?

To Hale, writing on the same occasion, he adds : —

"One half of our circle have now passed within the veil, and it grows more and more transparent. The Beyond seems not the Far-off, but a near and present home of the spirit, filled with spiritual presences. They go that they may no more be absent."

TO SAMUEL JOHNSON.

FALL RIVER, June 26, 1851.

DEAR SAM, — You are right. The words of Jesus are not yet obsolete, because his work is not yet fulfilled. The Truth comes not to bring peace, but a sword. This antislavery question comes, as Christianity came, into an unbelieving age; comes judging, dividing, separating family, church, political party, precisely because it is the question which now in this country tests the fidelity and sincerity of individuals, and church, and party. And therefore you are right in holding your ground, feeling that the question is one quite beyond persons. We do not doubt what the result will be in the end. And the end will come the sooner, and bring the peace which shall endure, the more faithful every man is in his place. Whether your friends are able to keep you at ——, or whether you shall be called to another place, — for a place you will find or make, — of this be sure, that *your* fidelity, dear Sam, is bringing on God's Kingdom. If we can but all of us say, " Father, glorify Thy name ; for this cause came I unto this hour ! "

At the same time, it is pleasant if one can have the peace and fidelity, too. I hope I have not failed in the latter. I have spoken plainly

and strongly, and I know there are some in the
Society who do not want to hear or have such
preaching. But I must do them the credit to
say that they have manifested no disposition to
interfere or oppose, and I believe the majority
of my Society would not be satisfied with a minister who should be wavering or wanting in this
matter. So that we have had no trouble on this
point, and, so far as I know, the "lukewarmness"
has not come of it.

After considerable delay occasioned by some
legal difficulties, the Society voted last Tuesday
evening to request me to withdraw my resignation, and to raise eighteen hundred dollars by
tax on the pews for repairing and putting in
order the house. And they have got enough
subscribed to pay all the annual expenses. The
crisis called the people out, and quite a strong
personal interest has been manifested toward
me. One man, who does not go to church and
whom I never spoke to, said he would give
"*five dollars !*" rather than have me go out of
town !

Mr. Longfellow's first settlement was, after
all, a short one. He had discharged the duties
of his pastorate with diligence and sympathy,
and with that unfailing sincerity which made all

his ministrations so fresh and real. He had
become interested in his people; to some, much
attached. He had entered heartily into the life
of the town, engaging actively in its philanthropies, and promoting its agencies for mental and
moral improvement. To the schools, especially,
as a member and as chairman of the school
committee, he had given much time and labor.
Yet a certain congeniality between himself and
his position, which was indispensable to his happiness and sense of fitness, seems to have remained wanting. He did not come to feel it
"his place." At the same time the business
difficulties of the church had continued; the congregation had not increased in numbers; what
seemed to him the "passivity" of the people
had not yielded to his influence so visibly as to
assure him of the value of his work among them.
As events showed, there was injustice to himself
and to his true success in the discouragement
he came to feel. "It is good to have patience
with a place," he wrote later, "and perhaps I did
not have enough at Fall River." But after much
misgiving as to his duty, he offered his resignation of the pulpit in the early summer of 1851.
It was received with warm tokens of regret;
and, as intimated in the last letter, was declined
by a nearly unanimous vote of the Society. His

own judgment, however, was not overruled by the regard manifested, and he insisted on withdrawal.

At about the same time, he received an invitation from a gentleman in Boston to visit Europe as tutor to his son. The opportunity attracted him, both as giving him a long-coveted privilege, and as offering him the prospect of improving his health. He therefore accepted it, and sailed for England in the autumn.

Before his departure, he wrote Mr. Johnson, encouraging his friend, who was also just leaving his pulpit, and expressing his feelings as to his own pastorate and its termination.

"I am sorry," he says, "that your departure from —— should be brought about in the manner it was. At the same time, I have not felt —— to be just the place for you because there were not enough people there for your elective affinity to choose such as belong to you. But a place is awaiting you. No fear but you will find it. Meanwhile, where you are is your place, 'heart within and God o'erhead.' It is not pleasant to uproot even a year's growth of attachments, but it is as true now as it ever was, that no man who has forsaken brethren and friends, or home, for the truth's sake, but shall have heavenly reward. The *apostolic* function is renewed in every earnest age. And he that scattereth is blest as he that reapeth."

"I felt very sorry," he continues, "to leave Fall River, in the depressed condition of the Society ; but it could not be postponed, and I trust to their finding some stirring person who will really 'build them up' outwardly without failing of true spiritual ministration. I found quite a regret at my departure on account of my connection with the schools, where it seems my services were esteemed, though I did not know it. One thing I shall have more faith in now, — in the influence that may be exerted, and recognized, from a very quiet person. I thought that, in a community like that of Fall River, a man must take an active part in public affairs, be able to speak in public meetings, and take the lead in movements.

"I have never regretted that I went there. It has been a good thing for me and I was very independent there. I should have been glad if it had proved the place for me, for I do not like transplanting, and with each year one gains power to do more in those which shall follow."

VII

FIRST VISIT TO EUROPE

IT was originally intended that the tour abroad of Mr. Longfellow and his pupil should occupy two years. But the youth's health became seriously worse, and within a year they returned. Great Britain had been visited, and they had lived nine months in Paris, "the place," wrote Mr. Longfellow, "which I cared least of all for. But it is a fine spectacle, a spacious, bright, and picturesque city, a well-dressed, cheerful, and quiet people. I admire the varied beauty of its streets, the grand scale of its public places, monuments, buildings ; the richness and hospitality of its libraries, lecture-rooms, and galleries of art. But it does not get hold of my enthusiasm, and, after all, ugly London interests me more than beautiful Paris." After their three or four hours of daily home-study, the tutor and pupil would explore the city together, seeing its works of art, and searching out the associations of its history in the rambles always so agreeable to Mr. Longfellow. But Italy and Germany were given up,

and they returned home with some disappointment, after a year which, to the elder of the two,
had been, as he felt, " little more than a wasted
one," except for some physical reinvigoration.

Mr. Longfellow's letters from abroad were
naturally interesting and graceful, but those
scenes are now so familiar that no extracts are
here made from his correspondence. His European tour was but the first of several, most of
them more delightful and profitable to him than
the first.

VIII

CANDIDATING AGAIN

THE thread of Mr. Longfellow's correspondence with Mr. Johnson is taken up in the following letter, which intimates his mode of life for a period of somewhat more than a year.

TO SAMUEL JOHNSON.

CANTON, December 26, 1852.

DEAR SAM, — If writing a letter be a meritorious work, as I sometimes fancy, in the present instance, at least, I shall claim no credit ; for I am fairly driven to it by lack of any other way of spending my evening. I am as effectually cut off from the usual resources of social intercourse as if I were in that veritable Canton where all talk is Chinese, and all books are printed in perpendicular columns of undecipherable characters. At this Massapoag House I exhausted the newspapers last evening, and find no book except Hoyle's Games, never very edifying to me, and especially improper for Sunday reading. My solitude is unbroken by any visitant. No hearer

of to-day comes to thank me for thought or spiritual impulse imparted ; no Cantonian lay-mon-
itor to unfold the true theory of preaching ; not
even the parish treasurer with his rumpled ten
dollar bill, — the faithful preacher's reward. For-
tunately, when I forgot to put a book into my
Sunday parcel, I did not omit my little cylindrical
writing case, and in these desperate circumstances
I turn to it, and in my solitude to you. . . .

A call to preach at Bridgewater gave me an
opportunity I wanted to visit the friends at Fall
River and New Bedford ; to the former place I
wended on the Monday morning, and so warmly
was I welcomed, and so urged to stay and so
invited to dinner and tea, that I did not get away
to New Bedford till Saturday morning ; being
obliged to withstand manfully all entreaties to
stay and preach. I found the outward and visible church with its horn verily exalted, — literally, inasmuch as the pinnacle, which lay so
forlornly prostrate and shattered when I left, has
been picked up and restored to its proper place ;
and figuratively, since various needful repairs and
alterations and paintings had been accomplished.
The exterior has assumed a fearful but popular
chocolate color called freestone ; the inside dreary
blankness of white wall is warmed into a neutral
tint more agreeable to the eye. I found the

"new incumbent" taking hold quite vigorously
of these externals, — he said the spiritual things
must next be looked after. . . . His wife is much
liked, and does wonders in visiting, etc.; and
both were very friendly *me-wards*. . . .

Since, I have been at Cambridge, have preached
at Woburn, have seen Clough, author of the
"Bothie," who has come over here to live, having had to give up his fellowship because un-
willing to take orders in the English Church;
and heard Thackeray's lecture on Congreve and
Addison, — a pleasant piece of literary criticism,
touching lightly and brightly along the surface,
but not sounding any depths ; with a pleasant
voice and quiet, gestureless delivery.

IX

THE BROOKLYN PASTORATE

As a religionist and moralist, Samuel Longfellow was a typical product of the transcendental awakening. The influences of that movement reached his receptive nature at a formative period, and found in it material peculiarly congenial. "He was," says Colonel Higginson, "one of the most consistent of its representatives, never having gone through contradictory and wavering *phases* as many others of us did. But this very fact shows the strength that lay beneath that gentle mien." Certainly it was always characteristic of Mr. Longfellow that truth which he accepted entered into the structure of his mind, and was thenceforth an integral part of his intellectual and spiritual being. Born into the clear but unstimulating atmosphere of the older Unitarianism, his mind, peculiarly sensitive to religious impressions, accepted quietly but earnestly its simple theological conceptions, as it did the moral principles of the upright but unaggressive people among whom he was reared.

The Unitarian Christianity of his early days had laid aside the absurd and revolting features of New England Calvinism, — a triune God; the original depravity of man; the eternity of punishment; vicarious redemption, — but it retained, naturally, the general conception of the relations of Deity and humanity which underlay all Christian creeds. God was a Being of love. The nature of man was good, not evil, — although individual men were indeed weak and erring. The earthly life was a period of probation, of which another stage of being would register the results, in joy or pain, according to a strict, if merciful, equity. Character was the principal thing. Distrusting elaborate doctrinal schemes, the Unitarians read the Gospels with more sympathy and satisfaction than the Epistles, and turned to them for guidance in life and conduct, relying confidently on Divine Goodness to direct in benevolence the issues of existence. They recognized in Jesus a Saviour, but this chiefly through the example of his conduct, the inspirations of his character, and the lessons of his lips; and they accepted from these an influence which, on the moral side at least, was marked and gracious. Orthodoxy freely testified to the personal rectitude which was its result.

But in their general view of divine things, as

in that of the Orthodox, Deity remained, in effect, for the Unitarians, a sovereign, outside creation, directing the affairs of the world not only by influences upon the hearts and consciences of men, but by revelations through the words of formal Scriptures, and by commissioned delegates, — above all, by Christ, his Son. The latter was, indeed, not Deity, nor had the Unitarians a clear and long-tenable philosophy of his nature. The human element in Jesus was gaining steadily in effective recognition. But he was the highest of God's creatures, and was deemed by most of the sect to have been preëxistent to the actual order of things. While human, he was also of divine quality, and he was authenticated to his brethren as God's emissary by the miracles which he wrought, and especially by his own resurrection and ascension. He would be, in some sort, their judge, as he was their exemplar. But he was *imitable;* it was possible to follow him, for man was by nature good and of free will as to conduct and motive. The supremacy of the reason the Unitarians also, and especially, asserted; yet they too often effectively, and half-unconsciously, limited its sphere of action to the interpretation of the revelation of fact and truth which they assumed as existent in the Bible.

Conceptions and principles like these, too largely intellectual, it may be, yet held with real fervor of conviction, and often made very gracious in the faith of the Unitarian people, of pious clergymen like Dr. Nichols, and saintly women like his own beloved mother, Samuel Longfellow brought with him to the Divinity School, little modified by the experiences of college training, as the outfit of his religious life.

But about the time our youth left his home, new voices began to be in the air. Channing, indeed, had largely prepared the way for a new order of conceptions by his magnificent vindication of the dignity of human nature. European thinkers and scholars were suggesting new principles in philosophy, and new methods in criticism. The nature of the Bible was beginning to be differently explained. Its origin was inquired into and its contents scrutinized more carefully. Its miraculous element was questioned, and by some referred to myth. The mind of New England was being leavened and emancipated by the thought of Emerson. "The Transient and Permanent in Christianity" were examined and forcibly contrasted by a fearless iconoclast. Some among the Unitarian ministers were soon preaching, quite freely, on natural principles of inquiry into truth. The title "humanitarian" began to be applied to a small number who asserted the nature of Jesus to be that of manhood, simply. A school of thinkers presently arose who declared of the prevailing theological view that the whole current conception of the relations subsisting between God and man, so mechanical and arbitrary, was unfounded and impossible. God is not outside the world, they declared, a monarch and law-giver. He is *in* the world. He *is* the world and all that exists. All things, all beings, are *in Him*. Man's relation to Him is immediate, depending for the knowledge of it only on the individual's power of apprehending spiritual Deity, of coming into conscious communion with Him. He is not a great personage, afar off on high. He is Infinite Spirit, all-present Being. He is the " Over-Soul," "above all, through all, in all." The truer symbols of Him, or metaphors of his relation to human spirits, are the circumambient atmosphere, invading every aperture ; the all-pervasive light, illuminating every crevice of nature; ocean's vast flood, pressing with each tide into all the rivers, creeks, or smallest rills that open to receive it. Man is God's microcosm, divine as He is divine, being his offspring. In man's self are all the laws of his being and life, and there to be studied. Know thyself, and thou knowest all things.

Virtue is health of soul. Rectitude is truth to self. Man needs no outward, formal revelation, nor is any such possible or conceivable. The Spirit expresses itself spiritually. Man requires only to become plastic to the ever-present influences of God. Thus he receives all truth and is helped to all progress. Jesus of Nazareth was no specially created or endowed messenger from God. He was only a child of God who had attained his proper heritage. He was the ideal man, type of mankind, become such through entering into perfect harmony with himself and God. If he wrought miracles, they were only wondrous manifestations of the working of laws, wholly normal, but inaccessible to impure or undeveloped souls. The church is the company of God's faithful ones, in every clime, who know Him and are banded together for his worship and service, — which is the service of truth and humanity.

Into conceptions like these, much of the best and most active spiritual life of the time was rising. They modified deeply the sentiments of many who could not wholly break with the beliefs in which they had been trained. But the change was slow, and especially to the well-established image of Jesus as the Christ, men and women clung with tenderest fidelity. Samuel Longfellow parted very gradually with the forms of thought and the pietistic associations which he brought with him from his home. In the Divinity School, he says, his views were more conservative than those of Johnson. It was chiefly that the cast of his mind was more sentimental and idealistic; that of his friend more purely intellectual. His growth was slower than that of many of his companions, and, as Colonel Higginson has said, more steady, without reactions. It was less conscious, because it was less by the intellectual and formal recognition of truth, with consequent conviction, and more an assimilation of it which made it a part of himself. His relation to Jesus was always that of a frank loyalty, full of veneration and admiring love, which never varied or waned. He retained, as we have already seen, through some years of his ministry, the Christian phraseology and Christian associations, and valued and used the Christian rites. As his views became more distinctly theistic, he gave to these traditions of Christianity new interpretations, which sufficed him long, but they became at last insufficient, and were gradually disused. Of his preaching at Fall River there appear to remain few relics. But, during that period, and the year or two of repose and reflection which succeeded it, his mind evidently developed in power, and his thought gained clearness and consistency. When Mr. Longfellow took up his Brooklyn pastorate he was in full possession of his religious point of view. His thought was henceforth only to expand according to its own well-established principles.

In January, 1853, he writes thus to Johnson, from his beloved Portland : . . . " After a month's wanderings, I had just come home, thinking to rest awhile under the old roof. But I have decided to take the week between two Sundays with Higginson, at Worcester, for the purpose of doing up the business of the seaside book [' Thalatta '], which I want to have over, it seems so trifling a thing to have one's thoughts busy about in these days. But for old love's sake, I would not have undertaken it.

. . . " I find myself very much unsettled, both as to plans for the future and doings for the present. The idea flits before me that I may go abroad again in the spring, to complete my tour. Sometimes I think of a free church somewhere. And then of a regular settlement in some pleasant town, with a gothic church and a parsonage. Sometimes I want to make a tour through our own country, visiting prisons and reform-schools, and sometimes dream of getting myself made chaplain in one of the latter, thus combining the satisfaction of my philanthropic and philo-pædian propensities.

" Meanwhile nothing is accomplished save stray Sunday preachings. I was last at W. I stayed with a man who talked of the 'indigenuous products' of the country, and of the abundance of 'empherial publications.' He said that in one thing S. was very unlike me, — it was very easy to follow him in his preaching! He referred, Sam, to a sermon of the simplest sort on Quiet from God! Has B. sent you a copy of his book? He hopes it may 'save some congregation from the *torture* of listening to the theories, the *experience*, or the *moral wisdom* of the man who stands in their pulpit,' etc., etc.

" To such words what can I venture to add? I shrink into initials and scarce venture to sign myself S. L."

From these uncertainties and crudities Mr. Longfellow was soon to be relieved by coming into the presence of the most important portion of his life-work. During the next month, February, 1853, he mentions that he is to preach for two Sundays at Brooklyn, N. Y., where he seems to have preached once very soon after his return from Europe in the preceding autumn. But he hopes the church at Brooklyn will call Johnson, whom he thanks for urging them to hear him-self. " Sam, do go to Brooklyn, if they ask you. It is such a place as you ought to be in. I don't know about that Society especially, but there must be a good element in it since they invited *you.*"

Just a month later, March 7, 1853, he writes : "I ought not to have let you learn first from the papers that the Brooklyn committee asked me to come again for six months. I said I would, with the understanding that I might leave sooner if I chose. I had really hoped they would ask you. But they are not yet ready for your strong meat. These babes in grace must be fed with milk awhile. I shall try, at any rate, to make it ' *sincere* milk,' Sam. . . . I don't see how they are to be satisfied with *my* preaching, after yours. But it was thought that I, in some sort, united, or might unite, the two wings. . . . It seems plain that the liberal party has the preponder-ance, and I am glad of that. . . . As to a perma-nent settlement, I had, and have, some doubts, first, whether I should be content to live in so decidedly a *city* place ; secondly, whether I should do for the place. I am so quiet a person, have so little of the 'popular' qualities ; am so little calculated to lead a ' movement,' — to make any *éclat.* Starr King seemed rather to be their ideal, and I am far enough from that type. But I thought it might be good for me to be thrown into a position making greater demands upon me. I may develop some new phases; at any rate, I shall test myself. An arrangement for a few months was, therefore, what I wanted. . . .

" Brooklyn is certainly a handsome city, and in the summer its neighborhood must be charming."

TO SAMUEL JOHNSON.

BROOKLYN, Tuesday, April 19, 1853.

DEAR SAM, — Just five words to say that I am in Brooklyn, and ready to receive communications. . . .

I " opened " with a rainy Sunday, — a storm from the East; not symbolical, surely, of my coming, — and in the old lecture-room, which, after all, suited me well enough, who like to slip in quietly everywhere. Next Sunday we expand into the new hall of the Athenæum, of whose size and consequent emptiness I am rather afraid, remembering how we were crushed at Fall River by our vacant whiteness. Sunday morning, Sam, I woke up the veriest coward. I was sure that I never could do the work that was wanted and expected here. I wondered why I had ever come. I was almost ready to run away and hide myself in the littlest village

I could find. But when I went to the hall I found friendly faces, and felt drawn toward the people ; kindly greetings followed, and by night I was cheered and hopeful. But I foresee many such alternations.

Four days later, Mr. Longfellow delivered his noble sermon on " The Word Preached," to which he refers in the following letter. The function and true position of the pulpit were never, perhaps, more forcibly, yet discriminatingly, exhibited and vindicated.

TO SAMUEL JOHNSON.

BROOKLYN, May 18, 1853.

DEAR SAM,—I am glad we published "Thalatta " because it brought me a letter from you. Do you know how inexcusably silent you have been ? I really began to have alarms as to possible causes. But who gave you such extravagant statements about "crowds in the new hall"? There are *some* seats left yet ! Still, the attendance is encouraging, both morning and —afternoon. Yes, I could not get the evening service ; but I think that during the hot months we shall have but one.

As to "popularity" I cannot say. One thing I know, I do not seek it. . . . As far as I can judge from my imperfect acquaintance with the Society, it means to place itself decidedly upon liberal and progressive ground. On our going into the new hall I preached a sermon upon the true position of the pulpit, especially in respect to free inquiry in theology and to reforms in society; and another upon the true Unity, to be sought not in form or creed, but in the Spirit, urging the society to take its position distinctly on the ground of absolute freedom; and I was glad to find they were willing to take this platform. At least, they wanted to print the sermons, and one gentleman who had been considered most conservative was most strenuous in this behalf. Perhaps you think that suspicious. I can't help it! I don't try to "please both sides," you *know*. I suppose my natural position is a *mesothesis*. I sometimes wish I had more "excess of direction," as Emerson calls it, and more enthusiasm. But I will not leave people in doubt on which side my sympathies are.

TO SAMUEL JOHNSON.

BROOKLYN, June 16, 1853.

DEAR SAM, — . . . At Cambridge was a pleasant dinner where Emerson, Hawthorne, Lowell, Clough, and Charles Norton were the guests. . . .

I did not get a sight of the celebrated A. U. A. Report; I fancy it was but a statement of the basis upon which the Association will carry on its operations, and of no bearing upon those out of the Association, — not even a creed of the denomination. My own connection with the Unitarian body is so slight as hardly to be worth the breaking. But, as you know, my real affinities are with the free men and churches. I want it to be so with my Society, and therefore wish they had not the name Unitarian. I shall ask them to change it, if I remain; but it is not a point upon which I could insist. . . .

TO SAMUEL JOHNSON.

BROOKLYN, June 29, 1853.

DEAR SAM, — . . . I went to Cambridge, and these good people took advantage of my absence to give me a call. I have not yet been able to make up my mind. While everything about the position of the Society is attractive and encouraging, I feel a strange want of energy and enthusiasm for the undertaking.

I have been physically out of sorts since I have been here. . . . So, personally, I don't feel a great desire to stay.

TO SAMUEL JOHNSON.

PORTLAND, September 15, 1853.

DEAR SAM, — . . . I have stayed all summer through at Brooklyn, save a run to the seashore now and then; the hot days I fled to lovely Fort Hamilton, which you remember. . . . Our good people at B. were just beginning to come back from summerings when I left last Friday.

They talk of an Installation. Will you not come on? I will have a "right hand," if you will. And do write me a hymn, won't you? I should have dispensed with the Installation, as seeming superfluous, but they have never had a minister ordained unto them, and I said I should leave it to their wish.

TO SAMUEL JOHNSON.

BROOKLYN, September, 1853.

DEAR SAM, — . . . The Installation is to take place the last Wednesday of October. Furness is asked for the sermon, but has not yet replied. *Can't* you come on? . . . Some have proposed that the "right hand" should be given by the president of the Society, which idea I like, but I do not know what will be decided. There was some hope of a liberal Orthodox minister of Brooklyn being inveigled into assisting, — not

Beecher but Marsh is his name. Then, with Chapin, we shall not be quite Unitarianized.

The Installation was celebrated on the evening of Wednesday, October 26, 1853. The manner of it was more conventional than the new pastor would have chosen, who always distrusted things formal, and would have preferred a simple service of welcome and recognition in which he and his people should chiefly participate, with perhaps, for personal reasons, a few of his dear radical friends. But for this the Society was, naturally, not quite ready. It was in the usual order of things that in this first important occasion of their history the neighboring Unitarian churches and ministers should chiefly share. Mr. Johnson was unable to accept the invitation of the Society to attend, nor did he send the hymn which had been so earnestly besought by his friend from his reluctant muse. Another friend of Divinity School days, William Henry Hurlbut, who had recently relinquished the pulpit through the changes of sentiment prevalent at this time, was represented in a hymn ; but among those who took part in the services, only Rev. Dr. Furness, the preacher of the evening, and, probably, Rev. John Parkman, of Staten Island, who read Scripture selections, were peculiarly in sympathy with

Mr. Longfellow's characteristic views. The other clergymen participating were Rev. Samuel Osgood, of New York ; Rev. Frederick A. Farley, D. D., of Brooklyn, who offered respectively the introductory prayer and that of installation ; Rev. Henry W. Bellows, of New York, who gave the right hand of fellowship ; Rev. E. H. Chapin, of the Universalist Church of New York, who addressed the people ; and Rev. William Hall, of Ireland, who closed the services with prayer. Mr. Longfellow composed for this service his beautiful hymn " In the beginning was the Word."

Thus was formally cemented a union which was to become a very close and perfect one. Hitherto the Society, organized within only three years, had acquired no marked character of its own. There were present in it the two tendencies at that time found in all Unitarian churches, — sometimes painfully struggling with each other, — the conservative and the radical ; and of these the latter had scarcely the preponderance. The congregation had, within the two and a half years of its existence, united in very urgently calling a man so typically conservative as Andrew P. Peabody (who had just received the degree of Doctor of Divinity, which was to become so familiar in connection with his venerated name). They had also called James

Freeman Clarke, Horatio Stebbins, and Starr King, all men of marked ability and elevated character, but neither of them of the radical and idealistic temper of Samuel Longfellow, — although Clarke in matters of social reform was equally advanced and earnest, and even more aggressive than he. But the aspirations of the Society were shown in their seeking among such men for their pastor, and there were in it a considerable number of men and women of superior intelligence and strong traits, who were distinctly progressive in their tendencies of thought, and ready to welcome and promote their new pastor's transcendental views.

When Mr. Longfellow began his temporary engagement, the Society was worshiping in a small and rather dismal hall. Its numbers also were small, but there were warmth and hope, and the new minister won his way rapidly to the hearts of his people. His preaching attracted much attention by its originality and vigor, directness and simplicity, and especially by its spiritual quality and its moral elevation. In theology he took, from the outset, a distinctly radical position. Not wholly disusing, as yet, the Christian phraseology or the Christian rites, he preached a pure theism, in which the associations of Christianity held their place only as illustrative of universal religion. He pretended little loyalty to the Unitarian denomination, to which he had, indeed, never manifested much of the spirit of allegiance since his mind began to unfold. Rather, on principle as by personal constitution, he was distinctly and strongly averse to organized methods in religion. He worked best and most happily by himself, and could not endure even the light harness of Unitarian associations, now growing lighter daily. But the friction was already great in the Unitarian body; quite a number of the most promising of its younger clergy were breaking away from it; and more troublous times were to come. It was not unreasonable, in one whose convictions were already so distinctly formed, to prefer an independent position. Mr. Longfellow would gladly have had his society take such a stand as Johnson's "Free Church" had just done, at Lynn, and that which his other friend, Higginson, had just established at Worcester. Justly or unjustly the Unitarian name signified to him not freedom, but restriction, and the attitude of organized Unitarianism appeared sectarian. The question between individualism and association in religious action has not yet been settled, and is not likely to be for some generations to come. At least in 1853, the position of its self-made exiles was not wholly unjust, although a more hopeful and conciliatory temper might have induced some of them to refrain from seeking personal ease, at the cost of weakening the structure of a religious body in which alone there was then any promise of realizing the liberal principle in organized relations.

The Second Society of Brooklyn, very naturally, did not assent to their pastor's suggestion that they should drop the Unitarian name and connection.   He did not feel it a vital point, however, and their relations began in a happiness which was only to grow as the too few years of their connection lasted.   In his quiet way, he proceeded with the presentation of his positive views in religion and ethics, and very rapidly and permanently he impressed upon his church those moral and spiritual characteristics which were dear to his thoughts of what a church should be, and imparted to it much of the free spirit which he longed to have it share.   He was almost never controversial, very infrequently calling up the positions of others for refutation by argument, but always preferring the simple statement of his own view, to make what way it might among the hearts of his hearers.   His courage was perfect because it was unconscious, a simple loyalty to truth which it was impossible for him to withhold.

But he shrank from discussions, and the eager disputation, almost inevitable for many years in the assemblages of the Unitarians, was abhorrent to him. While, therefore, his church continued to maintain its place in the denomination, he associated sparingly with the clergy even of his own neighborhood, and took no part in the practical measures of the Unitarian communion, or in the hot debates which were simultaneously arising.

His advanced theological position, and his view of the true bond of religious union, Mr. Longfellow had clearly presented at the outset of his temporary engagement as minister of the Brooklyn Society. His first sermon after his installation was a sequel and fitting pendant to the earlier discourses. It was the keynote of his ministry. He entitled it " A Spiritual and Working Church." It defined and luminously portrayed a particular church as a "society of men, women and children associated by a religious spirit for a religious work." That in his definition he should have included *children* was a token of one of his warmest sentiments, but it also intimated the breadth and completeness of his conception. Youth was not merely in the tutelary charge of the church ; it was an integral part of it. He expected the church to have an elaborate organization for practical services to society, and some of the agencies

for moral and philanthropic work which have
since become most important in our churches
were anticipated in the suggestions of this discourse.   The Sunday-school, the study of the
Bible and of theological doctrines and questions
in religious philosophy, the printing of books
and tracts, the instruction of neglected children,
should be a part of its regular activities.   He
would have its members study together such
questions as pauperism, drunkenness, crime, slavery, and take active part in social reforms, as
well as in benevolent efforts.

It is interesting to note here that Mr. Longfellow was by no means wanting in a sentiment
for the church in its large sense.   His individual-
istic attitude, while doubtless congenial to his
retiring nature, did not indicate a willing isolation
from other religious souls, nor the lack of human
sympathy, which then, perhaps, marked some
independent minds, especially those of a narrowly
intellectual cast.   It was, practically, the enforced
position, in his time, of one fully possessed by
convictions like his ; or rather, it was a just illus-
tration of the *true* attitude, as Mr. Longfellow
saw it, of each religious individual mind, — that
of strict mental independence, the religious spirit
being the true bond by which one is united to
other children of God.   He speaks somewhat

wistfully of the unity in which the Roman Catholic Church seems to associate its members. It claims to make them "sharers in a general spiritual life, transmitted only through itself. They are not only recipients of the divine grace that resides in its sacraments, but sharers in the virtue of its saints and martyrs." "I have sometimes felt," he says, "that, amid the isolation of our individualism, I could envy the churchman his sense of membership in a great body of brave and consecrated men and women. I could appreciate the strength and impulse it might be to him to feel that he was one of such a host, and to look back and around upon the long line of those who had marched under the same banner, the sight of whose folds had nerved so many hearts for victory, and lighted up so many eyes filming in death." But this yearning toward the Church Universal could really be satisfied only by its broadest interpretation, which includes not Christendom only, but all humanity, that "Church of the race, — man in his religious relations, — which is founded on the grand idea of God which lies at the root of all the various conceptions of God."

The conception of a church as he proceeds to set it forth is strictly a religious one. It was, with Mr. Longfellow, no mere lectureship or academy, as some would have made it, nor even a mere philanthropic association. The functions of these were included in its scope ; but, characteristically, the church existed to develop in men the consciousness of God, and of their relation to Him. "A church must justify its existence by this, that it holds as its special thought — not its exclusive possession, but its special thought — the idea of God. This it is to apply over the whole domain of life. With this it is to meet all private needs and confront all public emergencies. By this it is to try all spirits, tempers, and aims ; by this to judge all customs, institutions, laws. . . . Its work is to make vital the thought of the living and infinitely present God, in the life of its members and of society." . . . Its piety "includes morality and humanity, as man is included in God."

Such an organization is held together, naturally, only by a "spirit, as distinguished from doctrine and form. Some creed or system of opinions about religion is almost universally the centre around which churches are gathered, or else some rite. Now, I do not deny that similarity of opinion is a bond of union. We are drawn to those who think like ourselves. But it is not the strongest or deepest bond. It is easily overridden by spiritual sympathy, or annulled by the want of that. Neither do I mean to undervalue correct opinion as making clear the way to right feeling and right action, though quite as often right feeling and action will lead to correct opinion. Nor do I deny their value to religious rites. But a unity sought in uniformity of belief, or of ritual or organization, is but superficial. Nor can it be permanent unless it destroy freedom and growth, and with them life. We must look deeper for the bond of living and abiding unity. And we shall find it where it has always existed amid the diversities of belief and organization, and under all their strifes, — in that unity of *spirit* which is alone the bond of an enduring peace. This unites, while creeds and forms sunder, and shut off as many as they shut in. Alien intellects are brethren here, and walls vanish."

Is not this the principle, the gradual approximation to which has actually measured the progress of the Unitarian body since 1840, and which is effectually working at present in the Orthodox sects to set them also free, and to realize among them the true church?

But no church exists merely for itself. This society of religious men, women, and children is organized for practical ends, for service. " To work with God, and for God, should be the great and consecrated aim of every church; to make its associative life contribute to the accomplishing somewhat of the Divine purpose ; to lend its aid to redeeming the world from its sins, its wrongs, and its wretchedness ; to reforming the age and the community from its special evils, and unjust thoughts, and institutions ; to advancing its spiritual elevation and moral purification.   In short, every church should work for the coming of the Kingdom of Heaven, the reign of justice and unselfish love, of freedom and peace, and holiness and brotherhood. . . . Nothing would be so sure to keep life in a church as its making itself a working church.   Nothing would be so sure to keep it filled with the Spirit.   Nothing would so bind its members together, nothing so surely tend to make them think alike, if that be desired, as uniting in common labors.   It seems to me that a church has no right to be, unless it can thus make good its claim.   The world has a right to put to it the question of the Jews : ‘ What sign showest thou that we may see and believe thee ; what dost thou *work?* ’ It has a right to expect from it wonders of feeding and healing and restoration.”

We cannot forbear quoting the eloquent language which follows, showing the high ideal that lived in this preacher’s mind of the institution he was set to serve : —

"It seems to me that whenever a new church is formed the angels in heaven ought to sing again, 'Now shall there be peace on earth and good will among men.' And God should say, 'Now is my Kingdom nearer, and my will more truly to be done on earth.' And Jesus should rejoice in spirit and cry, 'Behold new laborers for the harvest; now shall men learn to love God with all their hearts and strength, and their neighbor as themselves.' And old prophets' hearts should be stirred anew, as they proclaim, 'Now shall men beat their swords into ploughshares, and deal their bread to the hungry, and undo the heavy burdens, and give justice to the fatherless, and break every yoke.'

"It seems to me as if, whenever a new church is formed, earth's suffering, sinning, wronged, and perishing ones should lift their heads, and a new hope light up their eyes, as they cried, 'You will help us, you will save us; in the name of the God you say is our Father, the Christ you say is our Redeemer.' And all good men's hearts should be gladdened; and earth's tyrants and tempters, and plotters of wrong and framers of unjust laws, should cower and tremble, as before a new moral force rising up to conquer them. Is it so? I will not doubt that every church does something to this end. But the whole creation

still groaneth in pain, waiting for the manifestation of the sons of God."

He thus, in concluding, expresses the principle
of organization on which he assumes that his own
society will take its stand : —

" We will take for our basis not a creed, but the
spirit.   We will agree to differ in our theological
opinions and beliefs, while we will strive, in a
common love of the truth, after higher and
clearer views of it.   Believing that only through
freedom can the truth be reached, we will put no
shackles on any, nor place any obstacle, even of
coldness or suspicion, in the way of freest thinking.   And regarding this freedom as more precious
than uniformity of belief, we will make it more
prominent than any doctrine.   We will assume
no responsibility for opinions, and impose none.
We may hold the most widely differing beliefs
about the nature of God's being, while we strive
together to deepen our reverence and love for
Him, to yield a more complete obedience to his
law, and win a profounder consciousness of his
presence and his peace.   We may hold, as we
now do, different views about Jesus, but we will
be united by a common reverence and love for
his spirit, and find in his life, however regarded,
redemption from our sins, and quickening to our
piety and our humanity."

We have not space to follow in detail the course of the ministry thus heralded. "Happy are the people whose annals are slender." There would be few striking incidents for us to narrate. Mr. Longfellow's temperament and all his methods contributed to a ministry peaceful in spirit and outwardly uneventful. It is perhaps sufficient if we say of the Brooklyn pastorate that it was the consistent development in fact of the principles which, in his opening sermons, he had laid down; the realization, in an encouraging degree, of the ideals he then and ever afterwards unswervingly held up. Always he preached *religion;* whatever his particular topic, its interpretation was a *religious* one. The sense of divine things, of the presence of God in human affairs and with the private soul, was constant and vivid with him. It was too sacred for fulsome and passionate expression. It impressed a reverential quiet upon his devotional services, and gave a subdued earnestness to his preaching, which was only the expression, in every variety of form and through every topic, of the one great truth of God. No subject of human welfare was foreign to his pulpit. On political and social questions he never failed to speak, as occasion arose, with frankness and fervor. Yet he loved best the simple themes of the personal and

inner life, of domestic and social relations, of
faith and conscience and mutual love and service.
To reveal God in the private experience ; to show
the divineness of common things ; the opportunities of the highest self-culture in the nar-
rowest and most ordinary conditions ; to fortify
rectitude and awaken piety and aspiration in
common hearts ; to check worldliness in the
energetic and successful ; to show the young the
nobler meanings of which life may be full, —
these were the instinctive and congenial aims of
Samuel Longfellow as a preacher.

In the pastoral relation his guiding purpose
was the same, quietly and unofficiously to diffuse
the same truths, to cultivate the same religious
spirit, as opportunities of influence were offered
him in personal intercourse with his people. He
had no formal methods. He shrank from, rather
than intruded, specific religious suggestions and
pietistic conversation not called out naturally by
the circumstances of the moment. But his mind
was dominated by the religious consciousness,
and he carried the atmosphere of it with him. It
shaped and colored all his thoughts, and gave
grace to his bearing and sweetness to a voice
which habitually breathed the tone and accent of
veneration. Where his testimony to religious
truth was invited or challenged, it was borne with

frankness and solemnity. Were the *substance* of religious truth violated, it could rise to abhorrence or even indignation. As the vicissitudes of life among his people offered particular occasions of influence, he brought them the consolations, the encouragements, or the rebukes of religion with a spontaneous, simple directness which gave them a convincing power over men's hearts. He was a sunny, refining presence amidst their joys, and made himself as a member of each particular household by the ease and delicacy with which he entered into its interests and happinesses. One who had known a heavy affliction said, "He came to me when I was utterly prostrated, weeping bitterly with my fatherless boys. He said not a word, but drew them to his side, with his arms about them. He did not ask us to pray, — I only knew that he was praying. He seemed to lead me with my children into the presence of God, and bring about us his protection. I felt no longer wholly desolate; I knew that Love was about me still."

Mr. Longfellow especially liked unconventional and familiar intercourse with his people. He was fond of "dropping in" at an evening meal, or for a passing call, often brief, to leave a friendly word or some kindly token. Flowers were as dear to him always as in boyish days, and conveyed for him many a message of affection or sympathy. Only knowing from a friend that in a certain house there was a young invalid near her end in consumption, he almost daily left a little bunch of spring blossoms, to her great delight and comfort. "On the anniversary of my great sorrow," said one of his parishioners, " he did not make me a formal visit, but early in the day he brought to my door some violets, and I knew that they meant he remembered what I was feeling, and that his heart was with me." With one friend, upon their birthday anniversaries, he exchanged clover-blossoms, — real or pictured, — to which some former pleasant experience gave peculiar suggestiveness. He loved to encourage a fondness for art and literature, and many a young person had the mind opened to these sources of delight and culture by an apt suggestion of his at a happy moment. The photograph of some fine picture or statue; a little volume of poetry or stimulating essays; at some fortunate opportunity, of religious writings; would be the means of reaching a receptive mind and heart with stimulus, or direction, or help.

The happy home in which Samuel Longfellow had been brought up left on his mind a deep impression of the sacredness of all the family ties. For the marriage relation he cherished a peculiar reverence, and, though he never entered into it, he seemed to apprehend by intuition its deepest meanings. The ceremony of marriage he always conducted in a manner original to himself, seeking to adapt its impressions to the particular occasion, that it might not fail of full significance. Of the other religious rites, he especially loved that of baptism, celebrating it in the broadest spirit, as a service of gratitude to God for the precious gift of a child, as still more a child of God, and of self-dedication, on the part of the parents, to the sacred task of rearing it religiously and morally. The communion service, which he maintained for some years after his settlement at Brooklyn, he conducted in the same spirit as formerly, as a memorial rite, calculated to keep alive the honor and love of one whom he always revered as of ideal moral and spiritual qualities of character. He at length discontinued the custom, however; not from any change of feeling towards it, still less towards its object, on his own part; nor apparently from an impression that it tended to become a formality; but rather, it would seem, because he had come to feel that its effect was too intense, — possibly, that it was difficult to prevent its influence from being of too mystical a character.

Naturally, Mr. Longfellow interested himself

especially in the religious culture of the children
and youth of his Society. He early prepared
with much care a manual of devotional services
adapted to Sunday-school use. He superintended
the conduct of the school, taking part in its
exercises of worship, teaching a class of adults
or older youth, and making himself well known
and dear to the children of all ages. He had a
happy tact in composing for them little addresses,
half sermon, half story, some of which remain,
and are very graceful and suggestive. He joined
in their amusements with full zest, enjoying and
promoting picnics and the winter festivals, which
he was full of expedients to make entertaining.
He possessed, in a singular degree, the art of con-
veying useful thoughts to the young, almost without stating them. " He attracted all boys," writes
one of his young friends of this period. " We felt
a curious confidence in his interest in us, which
boys always appreciate and repay in affection
to their elders." Getting this hold upon their
hearts, his influence flowed out to them sponta-
neously, as religion, or morals, or good taste, and
won its own way. He did not, by any means,
limit his sympathy to the children of his own
church circle. " That kind gentleman," a little
fellow called him, who knew him, but did not
know his name.

An innovation of a wholly original character was presently devised by Mr. Longfellow, which not only established itself in the worship of his own church, but spread, seldom in so perfect a form as his own, to others. At the outset he had proposed to his people to substitute an evening service for the afternoon one then usual. At length they yielded to his desire and he prepared a novel order of service, chiefly devotional in its aim, and in which music was the leading mode of expression, to which he gave the name "Vespers." By this time the Society was established in its permanent church home, and with sympathetic, highly-trained musicians, the new form of worship was made very beautiful and very impressive. He yielded to the wish of his people in admitting anything in the way of a sermon, and this he reduced to a meditative address, the devotional quality of which, in his hands, harmonized it with the occasion and saved the unity of effect at which he aimed. His own taste and deep feeling were largely a condition of the full success of the Vespers, which, while a pleasing relief to the old reduplication of the morning service, were seldom elsewhere so impressive, or seemed so genuine as a devotional act. They needed, for their perfect effect, the influence of a leader with whom worship was an habitual mental attitude, and who combined with the instinct of religion the art of a poet and of a musician. Mr. Longfellow consulted with his choir over the details of each service, carefully selecting and adjusting the musical pieces, and the scriptural and poetical selections. Responsive exercises were at the time almost unknown in Unitarian and other Congregational churches, and became common at the suggestion given by these services of the Brooklyn Society.

The Vesper service-book was republished in many editions. The order was very simple, consisting, besides music, almost wholly of selections and adaptations from Scripture. Mr. Longfellow introduced several exquisite evening hymns from the " Roman Breviary." Two, at least, of these paraphrases were his own, the now familiar "Now on sea and land descending " and " Again as evening's shadow falls."

Early in 1857 there began to be suggestions of a project of the society which was very interesting to Mr. Longfellow, both for its practical importance and because it gave scope to his artistic tastes. It appears first in the following letter : —

TO SAMUEL JOHNSON.

BROOKLYN, May 4, 1857.

DEAR SAM, — You are a wretch ! and Mrs.
Jackson [1] thinks so too, though she does not use
that expression.

By a wretch, I mean a person, or a "party,"
who goes back to Salem and simultaneously to
silence. I fear it is even *Nirwana*, and that I
shall no-more-sea you. Write, write, Sam, and
convince me that you are not absorbed and
annihilated. I should be sorry to think of you
yet, or ever, as one who comes not again.[2]

As you don't take the " Inquirer," you probably
don't know that " Rev. Mr. Longfellow, pastor of
the Second Unitarian Church, has had an attack
of the varioloid, but is now convalescent." We
had a regular siege of six weeks. Three weeks
of varioloid, then as I was getting out, an attack
of lumbago and three weeks more, all leaving
me with weak eyes and a weak throat. Now
I am as well as ever, saving a little hoarseness.
The worst was, that good, devoted Mrs. Jackson

---

[1] The lady with whom he at this time boarded.

[2] Johnson parried this thrust in a letter of a few days later :
"Nirwana, let me tell you, for I wish maliciously to spoil that
heartless joke of yours, does not mean 'no-more-sea' (or see !),
but 'no more blowing of wind.' So please blow no more wind
at me ! "

caught the sickness and suffered more than I,
but she, too, is well again.

Perhaps you have, also, not heard that the
Second U. S. of B. propose erecting an inexpen-
sive chapel. This they have been supposed to
be doing at any time during two years past.
Now they have begun subscriptions. The money
does not come as fast as we should like, but we
don't despair. . . .

You should see the new study !

In another letter he gives more details. The
building — " chapel," Mr. Longfellow always
preferred to call it — " is to be in a simple Nor-
man style, of brick and Caen stone," to " hold six
hundred people," and to cost $13,000, the land
being $2,000 more."

In February, 1858, he is able to write that the
chapel will soon be dedicated, and he beseeches
Johnson for a hymn. "Do not disappoint us,
but seek the mood and let the thoughts and feelings sing themselves." "The chapel," he adds,
" with some things that might have been better,
is yet very charming ; open, social, simple, and
fair." In fact, owing to the financial stress of
the time, it had become necessary to curtail the
plan of the building in some important respects,
although its final cost was far greater than had

been intended. The material ultimately employed was wood, and a lowered roof impaired the beauty of the interior. But it was cheerful and hospitable, and after their long abode in hired halls it was a joyful event to minister and people to enter into a church of their own.

The dedication was celebrated on the evening of March 2, 1858. The exercises were simple, freed largely from the formalities with which the congregation were not quite willing to dispense, four years before, on the occasion of the installation. They and their pastor conducted the service, he preaching the sermon. It was at once transcendental, yet intensely practical, — if it be practical to exhibit the most elevated truths as applicable to the whole tenor of men's actual lives. Its theme was "The Doctrine of the Spirit," intimated by Paul in his great saying in the Epistle to the Ephesians, "One God the Father of all, who is above all, and through all, and in all." Substantially, the discourse was a vindication of the reality of the spiritual world and spiritual relations ; of the intimate presence of God in the outward world, in human affairs, and in receptive hearts. By a contrast, then less familiar than it has happily become, on the one hand with the crude metaphysical conception underlying the old theology, of a God outside the universe, directing its concerns by arbitrary methods and laws, and on the other hand with the ground taken by the positivists, who, dealing only with phenomena, find no God at all, it asserted, on the testimony of human consciousness, the absolute, infinite spiritual Deity ; One not as individual, but as universal. "Our spirits teach us of spirit ; and our spirits, if we trust them, will, out of their very limitations, rise to the idea of the unlimited and infinite. . . . Let us think of God as the all-pervading life, the all-embracing energy ; which lives at every point, and wherever it lives is thought, is love, is spirit, and so is person. He, the Infinite, contains and embosoms all. He, the Absolute, is the ground and being of all ; without whom nothing could be, in whom all things are, and from whom all things continually proceed. The laws of nature . . . are but the uniform method through which the forces of nature act ; the forces of nature are but one force, one power, — the Almighty God himself. He is not outside the world, but at its centre . . . always present in it, always creating it, the life of all life, the ever-present cause of all motion, . . . a Spirit everywhere, a present power.

"Oh, with what sacredness does this thought of 'God, through all' invest the world ! We walk amidst miracles. Every spot is holy ground. The distinctions of sacred and profane disappear. Nothing is common or unclean. How noble ought our lives to be in such a world! How sacred our daily work! . . . We are working among materials and fabrics whose very atoms are held together by the present power of God.

" But are we to accept this spiritual philosophy in regard to outward nature, and go no further? . . . Shall these mute, impercipient material forms . . . be informed by the Spirit, and shall we for a moment hesitate to believe and declare that God must much more dwell in his loftier work, his nobler manifestation, the human soul? . . . No; . . . made in his image, to the world of spirits like ours it is given to be a perfecter manifestation and revelation of God than all the lower Universe can be. . . . Through this spiritual nature man is a child of God, the Father. As child of God he shares his nature, is of the same substance with Him, — ' consubstantial,' as the old theologians used to say, — is therefore capable of being inspired by Him. . . . Our relation with God is in no sense mechanical, but purely vital. . . . Inspiration and revelation, therefore, are normal and necessary facts. God's spirit is but God himself, man's spirit is man himself. . . . In our highest spiritual action, the divine

and human are not distinguishable. . . . Wherever
God's Spirit is, there is inspiration, and wherever
truth is opened to any mind, there is revelation.

"This is thoroughly *Christian* doctrine. In
Jesus we recognize a soul which by native purity
and spirituality, and by voluntary consecration
and obedience, was opened, unclogged, and transparent to the inflowing and transmission of the
Eternal Light. His soul, quickened of God, was
in turn 'a quickening spirit' to the souls of men,
and is so still. In this way he was mediator,
though not *sole* mediator; son of God, though
not the *only* son of God. . . . His inspiration was
not peculiar in its nature; was special only in its
degree and quality. It was not arbitrary, but
came from obedience to conditions. . . . What
was actual in him is possible to all souls *after
their quality*. . . . Christianity, if it means anything, means this : the possibility of a vital, intimate union of God with the human soul.

"It is interesting to note how every awakening of fresh, religious life in the world has begun
with the proclamation of this central, vital truth,
— the essence of all religion, — the proclamation
of a living God, a present Spirit. . . . Wherever
this has died out of the faith of men, its place
usurped by the tradition of a Spirit that has been,
of a God 'retired behind his works,' of inspiration

foreclosed and prophecy shut up in a book, then when worship has become untrue, and life profane and irreligious, some new prophet has been stirred to utter anew the old, eternal word, God is, GOD LIVES ; now, here, within you, He moves, He speaks ! To-day, if ye will hear his voice.

. . . " So every great movement of moral reform begins with a proclamation of God's law written in the conscience, and of a present judgment.

" And to-day, friends, if we would have life in our churches, if we would stay this desolating flood of materialism, this demoralizing prevalence of dishonesty and compromise, and kindle anew the dying flame of faith in human rights, we must preach, first and last, the Holy Spirit THAT is, the Living God, who has to do with the affairs of men as intimately now and in this, as in any past age or land ; whose word our highest thought is ; whose will is found in our highest sentiment of right, which we must not dare to disobey ; a God whom we must not attempt to leave out of anything that we do ; who is infinitely near to inspire, to redeem, and judge us now ; from whose presence we cannot go, for that presence is in us and in all ; the central pervading and encompassing Force, — yes, and the embosoming Love, the in-working Justice, — condemning and bringing to naught all that is not of his Spirit and after his law; saving, establishing, giving victory and eternal life now to whatever is his own."

Only two more years passed for Mr. Longfellow in the proclamation of truths like these to his Brooklyn congregation. Even at the date of the dedication he was physically weary and unwell. He wrote afterwards to Mr. Johnson that he would gladly have laid down his service even earlier, but could not leave his people while they were struggling with the problem of permanently establishing the society and securing their new building. But he was longing for change and rest, and when the congregation was well housed and at home in the new "chapel," he felt that he must take a long period of repose from work. "Now they are tolerably prosperous and well established, and ought to be able to go on by themselves, and find a minister whom they will like as well or better than me."

This would have been almost or quite impossible, it would seem, for the large majority of the Society. Yet it is a part of the truth of those times, infected with the moral corruption of which Mr. Longfellow had spoken in the dedication sermon, — the "great atheism which went from end to end of this land," with "its endless compromise and servility," — that even among his own progressive and thoughtful people there were some who had been disturbed and even angered by the bold assertions from their pulpit of the "higher law," which politicians were then flouting; its earnest protests against the sin of slavery, and warnings of the evils to arise from complicity with its wickedness.

What surprises one now is that discontent with such righteous utterances came by no means always from the corrupt and reckless of our Northern communities, but often, as in Mr. Longfellow's congregation, from some of the best people, so blinded was that generation. "You will be surprised to hear," he writes to Mr. Johnson in January, 1860, "and disappointed, as I certainly was, that a sermon which I preached upon John Brown gave offense to a number of my congregation. I believe three families have left us. . . . I was charged with doing all I could to break up the Society, with destroying my influence, etc. O ye of little faith! . . . Certainly the truth must be preached but the more thoroughly! 'What is the chaff to the wheat? saith the Lord.'"

The tenor of the John Brown sermon may be gathered from the following letter of Mr. Longfellow's to one of his congregation who requested a copy of it.

BROOKLYN, January 11, 1860.

MY DEAR MISS B., — My sermon on John Brown was not written out; and the manuscript would be of no avail to you.

It was a hearty tribute to the noble qualities and aims of the man; a man of qualities rare in these days, and therefore needing to be honored in pulpits, especially while men of mere talent are eulogized.

I spoke of him as a man brave, honest, truth-telling, God-reverencing, humane, — a lover of liberty.

In the presence of such genuine virtues, one would hardly have the heart to blame the methods, even. So I simply said that his method did not seem to me to be wise, or the best. As an *ultra* peace man I deprecate the use of destructive force even to secure great rights. But the *world* believes in the weapons of war, and they who honor the heroes of the American Revolution have no right to blame John Brown because he used weapons of war in the last necessity.

Before the earnestness of such a martyr spirit, I feel how little most of us are doing and suffering in behalf of the slave.

My sermon, I am sorry to say, was not cordially received by my people. I was suffering under physical depression, and did not do justice to my own feelings. Yet there was not a word which I wish to take back, — but only to say more strongly.

I feel that most momentous times are opening upon us. It seems to me like the time before the breaking out of the Revolution. I do not doubt the result. God give us heart to be faithful. . . .   Truly yours,   S. L.

It is, perhaps, not surprising that any expression of admiration and sympathy for a soul so heroic yet erratic as that which dwelt in the person of John Brown should have been misunderstood in a most critical time, when men at the North were alive with anxiety at the possibility of war, and should have been deemed an indorsement of the "grand old fanatic's" quixotic undertaking. Nor would the friction from such sources have occasioned Mr. Longfellow's resignation of his pulpit, had not personal reasons been in themselves controlling. He had the support, in his antislavery views, of a large proportion — perhaps the majority — of his congregation, and the respect and affection of all. The Society had taken an impress from his character and thought which, under congenial successors, it was never to lose. But he had labored as long as in justice to himself he could, and was entitled to release. On June 24, 1860, he preached his farewell sermon, from Deuteronomy xv. 1 : "At the end of seven years, thou shalt make a release." "It was a noble exposition," says his latest successor, "of his views and feelings on the greatest themes. . . . Then they were the views and feelings of a little company, now of a great and ever-greatening host. It had been a ministry," adds Mr. Chadwick, "of wonderful refreshment, beauty, tenderness, and spiritual grace." In his final review of it Mr. Longfellow identifies the central thought by which it had always been inspired and shaped : "the intimate nearness of the living God, the Universal Spirit. . . . I have found that my preaching, beginning from this, would perpetually come back to it. Whatever topic of thought or life I would unfold, *this* was found lying at the heart of it. Was it some truth, his being was the ground of it. Was it some duty, his will was the obligation and the power of it. Was it some trial, it was his opportunity ; some grief, it was the opening into his peace. Was it life, it was to walk in communion and service with Him. Was it death, it was to go on with Him to communion and service beyond. This great thought seemed thus to radiate into every direction and path of life, and all paths led back to it.

"Thus it has been the centre of my preaching, — the thought and name of God. Others would put Christ there.   I could not put him there, for I found there always a greater than he."

He proceeded to a luminous review of his teachings in regard to human nature, Jesus, immortality, the Bible and the nature of religion; explaining the grounds of his dissent both from Orthodoxy and from some of the controlling Unitarian conceptions of the period.   His exquisite and discriminating characterization of Jesus would now well express the view prevailing among Unitarians, nor could anything more profoundly appreciative be uttered. "By so much as you remove Jesus from humanity in your thought," he concludes, "by so much you remove him from men's comprehension and so from their needs. But call him MAN, and in that name include that indwelling of God which is the native privilege of spiritual humanity, and you speak plainly the truth which the creeds have been stammering, and throw clear light upon the nature and destiny of all men.   Say that Jesus was God manifest, — Incarnate Deity, — if you will; but do not fail to say that *every* consecrated, obedient, illuminated son of man is, in precisely the same sense, in however different degree, the same. 'Whosoever is led by the Spirit of God, the same is the Son of God.'"

Two other characteristic passages of this noble discourse we append : —

" With such views of man and of God, and of their intimate relation, my views of life have been cheerful and sacred.   I have ever urged upon you this sanctity of life in its small as well as its great occasions, in its work and its play as well as in its prayer and its sorrow.   This world thus becomes one mansion of our Father's house, full of his beauty and his presence, our childhood's home; and not an exile, a prison, a hospital, a vale of tears, and journey to the tomb ; not even a mere probation and preparation for another world.   Life a noble opportunity for spiritual and manly growth and the doing of good ; heaven and its angels close to us, if we will see and hear; and death but the passing on, in the unbroken continuity of our being, into a life beyond, whither we carry all of ourselves unchanged into fresh opportunities and fresh influences.   That the life beyond is the simple continuation of the inward life here, I have felt a growing conviction ; the same essential character, the same spiritual laws, the same Man and the same God.   But I have had more to say to you of the present life than of the future, deeming it *now* of more importance."

"And I have always urged upon you Righteousness as an essential part of Religion. I have wished you to feel the insufficiency of the devoutness which was not an inspiration to rightdoing. I have urged you to cultivate Conscience, and feel the sacred · obligation of Duty, and the supremacy of the Divine Law, as revealed within you. I have urged honesty, integrity, veracity, as a part of your religion ; and pressed the claims of a high moral standard amid the demoralizations of this exciting life. And not only private morality, but the claims of society ; that you should add to its justice, and help its humanity, and aid its reformations till that kingdom of heaven be come, wherein their rights shall be given to man, to woman, to child ; to the poor, the tempted, the criminal.

"And I have not failed to urge upon you the claims of national Righteousness, without which no people can be free, can be strong, can be truly prosperous. Against the great immorality of our nation, its great disobedience to the divine law, Slavery, I have not failed to utter my protest. I have urged upon you the critical character of this question among us ; how the liberties and moral life of our land are involved in it ; yes, and the personal manhood of every one of us. Of its barbarism and its despotism I have not failed to speak ; of its frequent and frightful cruelties, and its essential and perpetual injustice ; that I might engage your heart and your conscience to work for the righting of this great wrong, the removal of which would ennoble and aggrandize every part of our country, and let it breathe its first full, free breath. Of the duty of the pulpit in this regard I have never felt a moment's doubt ; but with me it has been a desire and a privilege, even more than a duty, to speak what was filling my heart and conscience. Nor have I ever seen what right politics in the pews, and commerce in the pews, could claim to silence the proclamation of National Righteousness in the pulpit. Some of you have not been able to sympathize with all I have said on this theme ; and some that were with us have, in the exercise of their unquestioned liberty, gone away from the hearing of this word. I would rather they had stayed and been converted. But I wish to say to-day that you have fully respected the freedom of this pulpit ; that through all, no persuasion or inducement has been addressed to me to do anything else than preach my full conviction of this matter. I am glad, and you are glad, to-day, that I can say this."

So ended Mr. Longfellow's too brief, yet faithful and influential ministry to the church in

Brooklyn. Persevered in through no little physical trial, it closed prematurely, and yet not
before a rich harvest was ripening. He had put
into it the deepest faith and feeling of his heart;
the richest fruits of his experience and study.
He had loved his congregation, had been much
at home among them, and parted from them
affectionately and regretfully, yet amidst the
happiness of most tender expressions of their
regard and their sorrow at his retirement. He
was to meet them often again, and always to
find assurance that his memory was kept green
and remained dear.

Speaking of Mr. Longfellow at the celebration
of the Society's twenty-fifth anniversary in 1876,
his lifelong friend, Octavius B. Frothingham,
said : [1] —

"He was a man of men, one of ten thousand,
—a man the like of whom for infusing a pure
and liberal spirit into a church has never been
surpassed; full of enthusiasm of the quiet, deep,
interior kind; worshipful, devout, reverent; a
deep believer in the human heart, in its affections; having a perfect faith in the majesty of
conscience, a supreme trust in God and in the
laws of the world; a man thoroughly well in-

[1] As quoted by Rev. Mr. Chadwick, in his sermon on Mr.
Longfellow, December, 1892.

structed, used to the best people, used to the
best books and the best music, with the soul of
a poet in him and the heart of a saint; a man
of a deeply, earnestly consecrated will; simple as
a little child, with the heart of a child; perpetually singing little ditties as he went about in the
world, humming his little heart-songs as he went
about in the street, wherever you met him. . . .
He was one of the rarest men; in intellect free
as light, having no fear in any direction, able to
read any book, able to appreciate any thought,
able to draw alongside any opinion; hating nobody, not even with a theological, not even with
a speculative, not even with a most abstract
hatred; he did not know in his heart what hatred
meant; he loved God, his fellow-men. . . . He
was always in an attitude of belief, always in an
attitude of hope, brave as a lion, but never boast-
ing, never saying what he meant to do or what
he wished he could do, but keeping his own
counsel and going a straight path, ploughing a
very straight furrow through a very crooked
world.   He was as immovable as adamant and
as playful as a sunbeam.   He wrought here, as
the oldest of you know, with a singleness of purpose and a singleness of feeling that knew no
change from the beginning to the end."

X

AFTER BROOKLYN

MR. LONGFELLOW sailed for Europe in company with his beloved Johnson, June 30, 1860. The story of this tour, so long as they remained together, was briefly told in the Memoir of Mr. Johnson, which Mr. Longfellow prepared after his friend's death in 1882. The summer was spent in Switzerland, largely in pedestrian travel. In autumn they passed down to Nice, and at the beginning of winter made their way to Florence, where they remained until spring, when Mr. Johnson started homeward through Germany, and Mr. Longfellow went down to Rome and Naples.

The most interesting incident of this period was the entire recasting, during a rainy month at Nice, of the hymn-book, which had continued an object of much interest, of frequent reference in their correspondence, and of intermittent scanty profit to the friends up to this time. But Johnson, especially, had long been dissatisfied with it, on grounds of doctrine. Even before a second edition was issued, he had written that he was dismayed to find that there were at least sixty hymns in it which he could not conscientiously use. These were, of course, such as attributed a peculiar quality and special authority to Christianity, and recognized a supernatural element in the personality of Jesus. Of such, the collection was now thoroughly winnowed, to the sacrifice of many hymns, in form among the most beautiful. Even the exquisite " Christ to the young man said," by Henry W. Longfellow, was scrupulously excluded. The places of some of those omitted were filled by new ones, either selected, as before, from many sources, or written by the editors, — some of them especially for the new book. In all, the revised collection embraced about twenty of Mr. Longfellow's and half as many of Mr. Johnson's acknowledged hymns ; but, besides these, a number of their own compositions were inserted as anonymous, from motives of modesty.

This purely theistic hymn-book, perhaps the only one of its kind, was published in 1864, as " Hymns of the Spirit." Poetically, and in arrangement, it may have been an improvement on the " Book of Hymns." But its doctrinal limitations were, of course, a bar to its adoption in many quarters, and it probably never reached so wide a circulation as the former collection had at length attained.

TO MR. R. H. MANNING.

VIENNA, October —, 1861.

I blame myself for not having, in all these months, sent any reply to your letter. I know I was very glad to get it and to hear your views at the time about American affairs, with which I heartily agreed; desiring very much that the Free States should be freed from the political and moral drag-weight of the South. I wonder if you are still a disunionist, or like Wendell Phillips now, a union-with-emancipation-ist? I am one or the other, I am not perfectly clear which. I suppose that to be a disunionist is counted rank treason now in the United States. I can't help it. I am not a secessionist. I count the Southern States to have acted in a manner utterly unjustifiable, politically and morally; both in their method of declaring themselves independent without political cause, and without consent asked of their confederates, and also in their seizure of federal property and outrage upon the federal flag, thus compelling the government of the United States to resort to arms, and so, by their rash unreasonableness and violence, driving the country into war. The government, on the contrary, acted with the greatest forbearance and moderation, which could not have been carried farther except upon the extreme peace principle that war is never justifiable. This, of course, the government did not believe, and, believing in war, I don't see how it could do otherwise than it has done. I don't believe in war yet; that is, I don't believe it to be otherwise than a very barbarous, cruel, and unjust way of settling a difference, or even of establishing a just cause. And what I have read of this war in America does not change my feeling. These skirmishes and guerrilla fights, from which nothing results but death; this shooting of single men with deliberate aim; this rejoicing over the number of the enemy killed; this burning of houses and the like, do not look even like the primal "right of self-defense" of which the " I am a peace man " people talk; and I am not yet prepared to put my peace principles into a parenthesis, as the ministers do. How it might be if I were under the pressure of the excitement at home I won't say. I remember that John Brown shook me a little, but not off my feet. However, granting war, I don't see how our government could do otherwise than it did. And the uprising of noble enthusiasm at the North looked grand to me, and the lavish outpouring of money in a people whom we had begun to fear to be growing to love money more than anything. A flood of self-sacrificing enthusiasm cannot pass over the land without morally enriching it. It would have been well if this same disposition to sacrifice money, or the prospect of it, to ideas had been sooner shown. If men in the last years would have voluntarily borne the temporary loss of business to which they are now compelled, for the sake of principle, the war might have been avoided, because the slaveholders would not have been led on by continual concessions, to that height of audacious exaction which has made them at last rebels. It would be a great shame and sorrow if after all this suffering and cost the great evil should not be thoroughly reached and eradicated. 'T would be best, certainly, that emancipation should come voluntarily from the *masters;* but if they cannot be persuaded, they must be compelled, in the imperative interest of the general safety. And, singularly enough, the war puts into the hands of the general government the exceptional power which in times of peace it could not venture to claim.

TO SAMUEL JOHNSON.

PARIS, February 20, 1862.

DEAR SAM, — Your letter reached me just at the end of my Berlin visit, which I prolonged a little beyond my first intention, partly through inertia and the difficulty I always have in getting away from any place, and partly because I was having a good time in that quiet, sober, drab-colored capital, which suited my taste very well, though I should like a little more picturesqueness. I did not learn so much German as I had hoped to do, and cannot yet dispense with the *Wörter-buch*. Still, I can read it with tolerable ease. As to speaking, I learned but little, having no German companions, but only Americans. I debated with myself about going into a German family, and decided that it might be more irk-some than profitable, considering the chances of not hitting upon pleasant people. With Mr. Grimm I talked English, as I think he understood it better than my German, and I could not very well comprehend his. I did not visit him as much as I should have done, partly because he lived a good way off, and the weather was gen-erally bad, and partly because his wife was a good deal sick. I had a very pleasant talk with her (or *from* her, for she does not understand English) the evening before I left. She told me about her mother's (Bettina's) statue of Goethe, and showed me a bas-relief of hers, full of the sweetest classic spirit ; two figures representing classic song and the Volkslied. Mr. Grimm was always pleasant, refined, and kind. Another German family which I became acquainted with only just before I left was the Mendelssohns, relatives of the composer. The young lady is a reader of Channing and Emerson ; and there is a brother-in-law, a hearty, kindly Englishman, a hunter of chamois and a reader of the " Times," who believes thoroughly in property and possession, and counts that, if a nation wants a seaport for her commerce, that is sufficient reason for keeping it, and that Austria is quite right in not giving up Venice. Also, that there will have to be a property qualification for the franchise in America, before long. I heard a few lectures and a good many concerts. I found, on counting the concert-bills which I had kept, that I had been to twenty-five ! — not to mention operas. I was in musical clover, you see ; but lest you should fear for my purse, let me say that nearly all were Liebig's twelve-and-a-half-cent concerts. I made the acquaintance, among other things new, of Beethoven's Sinfonie in B-dur, — the Fourth I think ; it is altogether lovely, and must

rank, perhaps, even above the Fifth. Then the
singing of the Dom-chor, some fifty boys and
half as many men, was something wonderful;
fine old church music, some of it very elaborate, with perfect unity and without accompani-
ment. There was also one concert of the Män-
nergesangs-Verein, a thousand and more voices
singing national songs, etc. How you would
have enjoyed this! Indeed, it is plain that our
winter together ought to have been in Germany.
And the climate proved not severe, but rather
mild; very little snow, but a good deal of rain,
and almost constant clouds; a little gloomy, it
must be confessed. By the way, do you remember a Mr. L., who used to be one of your congregation? A son of his, a youth of seventeen, was
my chief ally and companion in Berlin. We
happened to meet every evening where I went
to get my cup of cocoa and read the papers, and
we became fast friends. I found him frank and
intelligent, with his head full of the new ideas,
as was indeed natural, his father being a hearer
of Parker, and his mother, now in the spirit-land,
one of the early abolitionists, a friend of Garrison
and Phillips. I lived at a very comfortable hotel,
pleasantly and centrally situated, for a dollar and
a quarter a day, including fire (in a high white
porcelain stove) and lights, and with a dinner of

eight courses! And have been in pretty good health, save something of the Florence trouble, and at the end a very severe cold, which still besets my lungs, and which I hope to get rid of in — Spain! Yes, Sam, thither am I going, day after to-morrow, with some twinges of the purse-strings, I confess (and premonitorily of the epigastric or splanchnic nerves at the prospect of a five days' sea voyage from Marseilles to Malaga). But I trust to finding a smooth Mediterranean, and believe that a hundred and fifty dollars will keep and bring me back to Paris at the end of the month, which is all I allow myself for seeing Granada, Gibraltar, Cadiz, Seville, Cordova, Madrid, and what lies between there and Bayonne and Bordeaux. 'T is but a run, you see, but I thought I should be sorry if I had not made it. I shall endeavor to make economies during my month of April in Paris. Then will come May on the Rhine, at Heidelberg and Nuremberg, which, unfortunately, I omitted when I was on my way to Munich, but cannot think of losing. Then through Belgium to England, and home perhaps in August, and then — . . . I begin to feel, Sam, as if I had almost too long a vacation. But what vacation ever made a school-boy want to work ? . . . By the way, at the last moment I came near losing Spain, after all, "for conscience's sake," Sam. For, on the morning of the day when I am finishing this, going to see our American Consulate for needed visa of passport, I am told I must take the oath of allegiance to the United States, and on reading the words of the oath, I find it includes a pledge to support " the Constitution without any mental reservation." Of course I could not do that ; and I said so, explaining my position about the Fugitive Slave clause. Finally the Consul, respecting my scruples, and seeing that the object of the regulation would be obtained by a declaration of allegiance to the government, waived the rest, and so I saved my conscience and did not lose the Alhambra.

How, at this fag-end of my sheet and no time for another, can I write of American affairs? I was glad to get your views. Our government cannot, of course, proclaim emancipation except where their army is present to enforce it. Nor ought they to do it, I think, without wise and sufficient measures to protect the emancipated, who would otherwise become the victims of their former masters, now exasperated by what they would think interference in their dearest interests. For the good of the blacks, I should much prefer that the slaveholders should themselves emancipate. Perhaps the government might do as the Russian Emperor has done, who, decreeing emancipation, has given the nobles two years to arrange the matter with their serfs.   I met in the railway train a young Russian who told me about them.   He said his family had arranged to give to each serf family six Russian acres of land, and to employ them to cultivate the rest with the payment of one third of the profits to the owner.   He told me that the nobles were about to ask or demand liberty and a constitution for the whole people, and to claim that the privileges of their own class should be extended to all citizens.   I told him I thought that was really noble.

In August, 1862, Mr. Longfellow returned to America, after what always remained in his mind the most profitable and satisfactory of his European tours.

TO SAMUEL JOHNSON.

CAMBRIDGE, September 11, 1862.

DEAR SAM, — How can I excuse myself for having been at home three weeks without having written you a word ?   I assure you it has not been that I have not thought of you often ; but you know something of my infirmity as to letter writing. . . . To-morrow I am going to Brooklyn for a week or so.   There is an autumnal convention. But I go more, you will guess, to see my friends.

This morning I heard Emerson at the Music Hall. It was good; not especially powerful. With all drawbacks, I think we can't but rejoice greatly at the President's proclamation. That little paragraph, that stands so simple, plain, direct, after the shambling introduction, — it is the death-warrant of slavery. Blessed are our ears that they hear! I should have liked that little paragraph all by itself. I should have liked the 1st of October instead of the 1st of January. But surely we can wait a little, and meanwhile, as Sumner said, immediate emancipation follows every advance of our army to every man who will come within its lines. Of course we should have been glad if freedom had come to the slave by the virtue of the North rather than by the madness of the South; by the free gift rather than the compulsion of his master; if it had been proclaimed as an act of national justice rather than a military necessity. But we know, too, that behind it all, as a divine law is working, so is a moral sentiment. Think of it, Sam, slavery abolished in one day! Could we have dreamed it, when we went over the ocean two years ago! John Brown just hung for attempting by arms that liberation which the President of the United States by arms now proclaims! Two years before, the army and navy of the United States joining to take back Anthony

Burns to slavery ; now army and navy pledged to protect the liberty of every escaping black man !

At about this time, Mr. Longfellow appears to have written the following interpretation of the symphony to which he refers in the last letter but one, which had so much impressed him, and which continued to be one of the musical compositions which he peculiarly admired.

TO MRS. G. L. S.

CAMBRIDGE, 1862.

Here is the story that framed itself in my mind as I heard the Fourth Symphony. You will see that it is an allegory of human life.

The call and aspiration of youth, postponed sometimes amid the joyousness of light-hearted days, and supplanted sometimes by the persuasions of religious quietism, hiding indolence under the guise of devotion ; forgotten sometimes amid the excitements of wordly "getting and spending," or the hot fever of sensual pleasures ; but still calling, and not always in vain, to the awakened and ashamed soul, which not too late grasps anew its early purposes and renders a saddened but redeeming service in the great battle of humanity.

BEETHOVEN'S FOURTH SYMPHONY.

I. ADAGIO ALLEGRO VIVACE.

A youth is awakened at early morning by the voices of his comrades summoning him to go forth with them on a holy crusade. At first their call mingles broken and vaguely with his dreams. But soon he rouses himself and joins them, and they set out, high in spirits and fresh in hope, gladdened by the clear morning air and the bright sunshine. A part of the troop press eagerly forward; a part linger in lively conversation, or stay to talk with the reapers in the field and with the blithe maidens who are binding the sheaves. Among these is the youth. And now, before he is aware, he finds that the morning hours are passed and the sun is high and hot in the heavens. The cool shadows of a pine forest invite him to turn aside and rest.

II. ANDANTE CANTABILE.

As he enters the wood, strains of sweet and solemn music fall upon his ear. It is the hymn of the monks from the neighboring Convent Chapel: —

In the world is sin and sorrow,
Youth to-day, the grave to-morrow.
All its toil is emptiness,

> All its hopes are hollowness.
> Life is short and judgment near,
> Come, thy soul for death prepare!
> Come, where holy saints have trod,
> Give thyself to prayer and God!
> Life hath danger, life hath fear;
> Here is peace, for God is here.

The youth yields his spirit to the soothing strain. He enters the chapel; he kneels in prayer; he loses himself in sweet and dreamy reverie. Suddenly the tones of a trumpet rouse him. It is the host of his comrades which, pursuing its winding way, is now passing the foot of the cliff upon which the chapel is built. Those tones recall him to the high purpose of the morning. He leaps up to go. But on the threshold a tender strain of music arrests him.

> Mortal, whither wouldst thou go?
> Vain are all things here below;
> Life has danger, life has fear:
> Stay, for Peace and God are here!

For a moment he hesitates; but again the trumpet sounds, already more distant, and he rushes forth to overtake his comrades.

III. SCHERZO.

His road soon brings him into the streets of a city. The host have already passed through.

But in the public square the crowd of market-day delays his steps. Unconsciously he loses himself in the eager stir of the buying and selling; he scatters his gold with the rest. The afternoon passes ; the lamps are lighted ; the sound of merry music is heard. A youth, crowned with vine-leaves, stands at the door of the inn and invites him in. He enters and joins the revelers. Girls with bright eyes and flushed cheeks bear him away in the whirl of the dance; he kisses their hot lips, he drinks with them the red and golden wine, he joins in their jovial songs. At last, overcome with the excitement, he sinks into a heavy sleep.

IV. ALLEGRO NON TROPPO.

It is broad day when he awakes ; he throws open the window to breathe the fresh air. He sees below him on the plain the host, gathering in battle array. The morning sun shines on their banners and their burnished arms, as they await the onset. Smitten with shame and re-morse, he renews his resolve. He hurries forth, hoping yet to be in time to take part in the glorious conflict. As he comes nearer, ever louder grow the confused sounds of the battle as it wavers to and fro. He rushes into the midst ; he seizes a weapon from a fallen soldier, — for

his own he has lost. The combat grows fiercer
and wilder, then there is a pause; the sounds
grow faint in his ears, the lines grow dim; he
has fallen, struck with a mortal blow. His
comrades bear him aside. The battle is renewed.
A shout startles his dying ear. It tells that the
field has been won. He lifts himself with difficulty, and with his last breath joins the cry of
Victory !

XI

OTHER JOURNEYS ABROAD

MR. LONGFELLOW visited Europe three times subsequently. In 1865, he was accompanied by a nephew, passing the winter of that year chiefly in Paris, and the succeeding summer in Switzerland. In the spring of 1868, he left America with two sisters, his brother Henry and his family, and Mr. Thomas G. Appleton, of Boston, and during more than a year's time traveled through Great Britain and over a large part of the Continent. The duty of directing the movements of the party and managing its business was confided to his somewhat unpractical, although experienced hands. His absent-mindedness and absorption in the beautiful or interesting scenes through which they passed led to some amusing misadventures. The number of umbrellas left resting against the trees of Switzerland, after he had concluded hasty sketches of its scenery, became a standing jest among his companions. But his enthusiasms surrounded all their way with a romantic charm, and to the

younger travelers their journey became an education in history, art, and literature. The associations of each place visited were made vivid by his
own eager interest and his familiarity with them,
and the pains and skill with which he arranged
the details of the tour to give them full and even
dramatic effect. In Scotland, with some of his
young relatives, he walked many miles to identify
the scenes of " Rob Roy " and "The Lady of the
Lake." In England, he led them through the
Lake region and to the home of Wordsworth, of
whose poems he was naturally a warm admirer.
The moment the party reached Florence, they
were carried, regardless of fatigue, to see the
Casa Guidi by the light of a propitious moon.
There, and at Naples, they traced the localities
of " Romola " and " The Last Days of Pompeii,"
stimulated by his lively imagination and his
excitement over some memento discovered, or an
engraving or photograph secured as a prize to
illustrate either novel. An occasional *contretemps*
afforded amusement at the cicerone's expense.
He had, long in advance, arranged their arrival
at Venice for the night of the full moon, and
great was his chagrin when they were welcomed
to the city by a pouring rain, and crowded into a
gloomy, covered omnibus-gondola for their first
voyage on the Grand Canal. At Flüelen, in

memory of William Tell, the children and their uncle purchased an apple, the seeds of which were ultimately to be planted in America. As their journey took them next day into Italy, they were not allowed to cut it upon alien soil, but had to carry it, with some inconvenience, for two or three weeks, until their return into Switzerland. There, with much ceremony, the apple was opened, and there proved to be not a single seed in it !

But he set to his young companions a finer example which did not fail to make its impression. "His interest was not only in the romantic and picturesque, but still more in present human concerns. Everywhere he had friendly chats with the peasant people, with the old vergers in cathedrals, and with innumerable young men and boys. At Lake Como and Sorrento he made friends with the young boatmen, and drew out their confidences about their business and home and love affairs, into all of which he entered with the most lively sympathy."

Mr. Longfellow's last tour abroad was one of some months in 1888. He was accompanied by a young friend, Mr. William M. Fullerton, in whose society he took great pleasure during these later years, and whose recollections of this journey are of the same delightful kind as those just described.   His familiarity with localities in Europe was thus extensive, but there remained regions, as Egypt, Palestine, Greece, which he wistfully regretted never to have seen.   His letters from Europe were, naturally, charming; full of appreciative descriptions of scenery, works of art, music, and meetings with interesting persons in many places.   Comments upon political and social matters manifest his deep interest in the condition of the European peoples, and frequent references to public affairs at home show that, wherever he roamed, his heart remained untraveled.   Lack of space has prevented extended extracts from a delightful correspondence, but the following passages cannot be omitted.

PARIS, November 16, 1865.

DEAR SAM, — I must tell you something of my week in England. . . . Sunday morning I went to hear Martineau at the " Little Portland Street Chapel."   But it was not the Martineau of " Where is thy God?" or, " Let any true man go into silence."   He spoke from the other side of his unreconciled mind.   It was a defense of tradition as the ground of religion as against argumentative reasoning and individual inspirations.   It was the ground of the churchman against the rationalist and the mystic.   I was

much disappointed. Conway says, however, that
Martineau comes out very finely at conventions,
meetings of the ministers, and the like; but why
should n't such a man commit himself, once and
for all, to his best thought?

In the afternoon I went to Westminster Abbey to hear Dean Stanley preach on Lord Palmerston, who had been buried in the Abbey the
day before. The crowd was very great, and our
seats were too far off to hear without difficulty;
but from what I heard, with the report in next
day's paper, it seemed to be as honest a sermon
as could be preached, I suppose, in Westminster
Abbey. There were open moral scandals in
Palmerston's life; no principle but expediency
in his politics. So Stanley said he should not
touch upon political aspects, and personal religion
he "should leave where our Church leaves it,
with that Saviour who is able to subdue all to
himself." So he went on to speak of his good
qualities, and the honesty was in the absence of
fulsome eulogy, in the disclaiming of any genius
or remarkable abilities, but praising only his
faithful and industrious use of his powers, his
uniform kindliness, his fairness to opponents, his
cheerful hopefulness, and his devotion to England. All which he held up to the imitation of
"young men" and others. Of course, I think

that perfect honesty required him, if he spoke of the man at all, to speak of everything; for the "Church" certainly has, if anything, a moral judgment to pronounce; and how would the old gray walls have been transfigured by that highest honesty, even beyond the glory of that jeweled rose-window through which the sunset shimmered, while the invisible choir of boys' voices poured forth the chants and hymns, which rose and floated and died away among the brown arches and forest-like columns! As we left the church, the organ sounded Beethoven's Funeral March, which is like the moaning of the sea.

Having heard Martineau and Stanley, I went in the evening to see and hear Carlyle in his dingy house near the water-side at Chelsea. He received us kindly, — a slender figure in iron-gray surtout, with iron-gray hair and beard, and a face all marked over with strength and shrewdness, and touched with tenderness. Apropos of Emerson's "Gulistan" (a most disappointing book to me), Carlyle poured out about Oriental literature, and told us some story from a favorite Eastern book, whose name I have now forgotten. Then the talk turned upon Palmerston. He said he was not a man of ideas or principles; there were things "the vulgar applauded, but men of deeper insight withheld their applause."

He was not a man to lead the people; such were few at any time; but he was kindly, and kept things well together, and when he should be gone, "many an uglier man might come in his place, and so I always said, 'Live on, friend, as long as you can.'"   All this and much more was said, in a genial, kindly tone, in strong Scotch accent, with an occasional hearty and pleasant laugh. But universal suffrage happening to be spoken of, he at once lost his good humor and his good sense.   "To give every man a vote is to make Judas the equal of Jesus" (!), — "*I* never had a vote;" then, growing more fierce at some mild protest of mine, he began to talk about the "dirty nigger," and "better put a collar on his neck, and hold him down to his work," etc.   It was melancholy.   Evidently on this point he is, as Conway says, simply a monomaniac.   On all others, he says, he is full of wisdom, information, and tenderness.   We were glad, therefore, to get back to Palmerston, and the pictures on the wall of Cromwell and the young Frederic.   He resumed his good nature, told an amusing story of some "evangelicals," who went to labor with Palmerston, in his last sickness, for the good of his soul, to whom he listened, hopefully saying, occasionally, "Go on, go on," but suddenly, in a loud voice, asking them to "read the sixth article." That number of the Thirty-nine, however, not proving apropos, they at last discovered that he meant the sixth article of the treaty of Utrecht, on which his mind had been wandering! — which rather disconcerted their hopes of his salvation.

I breakfasted with Conway. Carlyle said of him to Brooks, " He is a very flexile person." He still preaches in Fox's Chapel.

SHANKLIN, ISLE OF WIGHT, July 23, 1868.

DEAR SAM, — . . . The house [Tennyson's] is so ugly, architecturally, that I have not been able to make up my mind to buy a photograph of it. Indoors it is roomy, homely, old-fashioned, and as "careless-ordered" as the garden. We passed through a vestibule, a hall with casts of Elgin marbles and a relief by Michael Angelo on the walls, and boxes of minerals lying around; through a staircase-entry with a bust of Dante, a medallion head of Carlyle, and numerous framed photographic portraits; through a sitting-room with books and pictures, into a large drawing-room lighted by a great bay window, outside of which on the lawn stands an ivy-clambered elm. There were tables covered with books, and on the walls were engravings, among them Michael Angelo's Prophets and Sibyls from the Sistine

Chapel. Mrs. Tennyson received us quietly and cordially, — a woman about fifty, with a delicate, invalid look, a tranquil face and manner, and great sweetness of expression and voice ; dressed in black, with something white on the back of her head. We fell into conversation, and, to my surprise, she expressed some timidities as to the enlargement of the franchise here (the new elections are soon to take place). " We should have preferred," she said, " that education should have preceded." It made me think of the old pro-slavery argument. Here, as with us, the felt need will bring about what no mere anticipation ever would have done. Education will go hand in hand with enfranchisement. Then she asked me to go out into the garden where Tennyson was smoking with the other gentlemen (H. W. L. having preceded us). She showed me through a study (piled up with books, and where the boys get their lessons), and outside its open window, upon the lawn, sat Tennyson, with a short pipe in his mouth and a large wooden bowl of tobacco at his side, under the shadow of a great clump of trees and shrubbery. He wore spectacles, and a high-crowned, broad-brimmed felt hat, looking just as when you and I saw him, and speaking in the same deep voice. There is something a little brusque, not to say rough, about his manner; yet it was kindly enough under all. They were speaking about *spiritism*, of which he seemed quite incredulous, yet interested in hearing about it from Mr. Appleton. When some one said, " I see you are bitten by it," he replied, " No, I wish I could be bitten by something; but I always stay in suspense, neither believing nor unbelieving." We went into lunch. Speaking of our going to the Rhine, he said, " I *hate* the Rhine. It is overrun with Cockneys. *We* went to the Rhine, and there came on board two fine life-guardsmen; they fairly reeked of Windsor soap. They washed their lily-white hands in the drinking water, so that we had nothing to drink. I *hate* the Rhine!"

After lunch he showed us all around the garden and grounds, and out into the fields under " the brink of the noble down." . . . He said he used to walk on the down, but did n't much now. Then up on the roof of the house to see the view, which is very lovely. Afterward he took part of us to drive upon the down to see the " Needles." I went again at seven to dine. His two boys were there, about seventeen and fifteen years. The oldest is named Hallam. I asked him if his name was also Arthur. He said, " No." I thought he was named from the father. The younger is Lionel, named from the constellation

Leo. Two very nice boys. During dinner the doorbell rang, and Tennyson exclaimed, "Who is that ringing the bell? Some wretched Cockney, I'm sure it is!" He seems to have, as Conway said, a perfect mania on the subject of Cockneys. He is building a house in Suffolk to get out of their way.

After dinner we went into the drawing-room, where the fruit was served, with wines and coffee. Tennyson said some pleasant things about waterfalls, describing beautifully some that he had seen. Then he asked us to go up into his den, which is at the top of the house, under the roof, with dormer-windows, and full of books. On the table I noticed a large volume of Lucretius, and a new translation of the Psalms. I told him that I tried in London to hear his friend Maurice. He said he had never heard him preach ; but one Sunday, when he was staying with them, he had read the service with great feeling, — "the only time," he added, "I have ever heard it read with any." "And think," said he, "of their turning *that* man out of college because he did n't believe in eternal hell! That's putting the devil on the throne of the Universe! The clergyman here preaches it. I never go to church. I used to go sometimes in the afternoon ; but hearing that the clergyman said I never went, I left off going. I could n't tolerate it. They gabble off the prayers so, and the sermons are such nonsense." He went on to say that there was a great shaking of the Church and of Christianity in these days. My brother remarking that the essentials of Christianity would remain unshaken, he said, "I don't know; the great central idea of Christianity seems to be that a god descended on earth to redeem man; that's what all the churches teach, except the Unitarians." "And yet," he added, "I can't quite take Renan, with his talk about '*ce charmant philosophe.*'" The conversation turning to verse, I spoke of his "Daisy," and its peculiar and exquisite metre. He seemed pleased, and said he had prided himself on the invention of a new metre, but none of the critics had ever noticed it, except to say that he had written a poem called "The Daisy," much inferior to one by Burns on the same subject! Then he said, "Can you read Boadicea?" and got the book; we declining, he began and read it through in the most astonishing sort of high-pitched chant, half guttural, half nasal. It was almost ludicrous, yet brought out the metre of the poem well. His boys then came up to say good-night, and kissed their father. After a time we took our leave, Tennyson himself lighting us out over the lawn and through the shrubbery to the lane, with a candle in his hand, like a glow-worm.

XII

EIGHTEEN YEARS IN CAMBRIDGE

In resigning his pulpit at Brooklyn in 1860, Mr. Longfellow no doubt felt that he was virtually retiring from the active ministry; at least, that he would not again become a settled pastor. The precarious condition of his health, and the not infrequent suffering to which he was now liable, constituted a practical condition which was nearly insuperable. A moral one, not less serious, was the difficulty of finding a parish resting on such a basis, in its organization, as he could conscientiously stand upon. His convictions and sympathies were deeply with those who believed that, in the interest of religious feeling not less than of mental independence, organized religion should be released from all theological restrictions and implications; that no doctrinal test, even the slightest and most remote, should be suggested by the relation of church-membership. Scarcely any of the Unitarian societies had, as yet, reached this position; and of other liberal congregations, distinctly based upon it, there were but few, and those mostly feeble and struggling. Mr. Longfellow could not resign the happiness of preaching where his thought was welcome ; yet he had little expectation of other than occasional or temporary services in vacant pulpits.

In fact, this was the form which his life took for many succeeding years. Living near or with his relatives in Cambridge, he preached, as occasion offered, in many of the Unitarian churches of New England and of the West and South. In one or two instances, his services were continued over periods of some length. In Newburyport, where a highly intelligent congregation had enjoyed the ministrations of his friend Higginson and of other progressive preachers, Mr. Longfellow was peculiarly at home. He supplied the pulpit there, at different times, for several months together, and returned to it on occasional Sundays, so long as he lived, to find the impression of his thought and faith unfaded, and an affection among the people such as one may be glad to earn in a settled pastorate.

But Mr. Longfellow's most interesting engagement was with the Twenty-eighth Congregational Society of Boston, gathered by the lamented Theodore Parker. Here a strictly free platform, wholly unembarrassed by creed or covenant, offered him a thoroughly congenial position. He preached for this society for more than a year, during 1867 and 1868, and very often afterwards, giving, especially, a noble discourse at the dedication of their new place of worship, the Parker Fraternity Hall, in 1873.

While these pulpit services called for the usual weekly preparation, there remained leisure for a variety of literary and æsthetic occupations. Mr. Longfellow, although he was unmethodical in his habits, had the art of filling his days with intellectual activities and refined amusements, with quiet philanthropies and kindly services of many sorts. Earnestly concerned to promote religious liberalism, he took much interest in the " Radical " magazine, and contributed to its pages some of his maturest thoughts. He was a constant attendant and frequent speaker at the " Radical Club," which was organized in 1867, and met for a number of years subsequently in Boston, and engaged in spicy conversation progressive and idealistic spirits like Emerson, Bartol, Alcott, Higginson, Wasson, Weiss, James Freeman Clarke, Wendell Phillips, Mr. and Mrs. Sargent, Mrs. Julia Ward Howe, Mrs. Ednah D. Cheney, and others.

Of the Free Religious Association, which arose about the same time, he did not become, formally, a member. "Why 'Free Religion'? 'Free Religious Association'? Are not 'Religion,' 'Religious,' sufficient?" But he was in full sympathy with the general aim of the organization, although he criticised some of its methods. He spoke at its meetings, and appeared often on its platform. His disposition to individualism seems also to have prevented his formal association with the various antislavery societies, although he was even a Garrisonian abolitionist, not only in his abhorrence of slavery, but in a willingness to separate from the South, on the ground of the pro-slavery character (as he viewed it) of the Constitution, and his skepticism of the possibility of a political union with the slave States which should not involve disgraceful compromise of principle and dignity.

For his enjoyments, music remained, of all the arts, Mr. Longfellow's chief delight and solace. He mastered no instrument, but he improved all opportunities of hearing music in the best forms then offered, and his knowledge of the science, and of its masterpieces, was extensive and thorough. Beethoven was his favorite composer. He especially loved oratorios and chamber-music. Literature was a resource which never failed him. He maintained a familiar acquaintance with the classics, and read habitually in the modern languages of Europe, not only studying their standard authors, but keeping well abreast of their current products in the departments congenial to him. Poetry was, of course, peculiarly his province, and whatever of it was beautiful in many literatures was familiar to him. Into his brother's literary work he entered with the deepest sympathy and appreciation, giving him occasional practical assistance in the preparation of his volumes for publication, especially those of his translation of Dante.

The relation of these brothers was one of the closest affection; a union of kindred spirits, bound by happiest family ties, and by a perfect community of tastes and sentiments. It was the blessing of the group of children who had filled the rooms of the ancient dwelling in Portland, that their mutual love was to persist unsevered, and to grow deeper throughout their lives. And, in this period of what must have been, in no small degree, one of disappointment in respect to his work in life, his enforced partial retirement from the activities which were dear to him was greatly relieved for Mr. Longfellow by the long continuance of his domestic associations. His intense love for children went out to the young generation who clustered in the homes of his brothers, and was enthusiastically returned. They confided to him without reserve their girlish and boyish interests, secure that nothing which concerned them would ever be trivial in his eyes. He was adopted with equal warmth and trust by their companions, and to all, indiscriminately, became "Uncle Sam." During several successive summers, parties of young people were made up, for jaunts in the White Mountains, or elsewhere, of which he was a most welcome member. "He was completely one of us, in our walks and drives and climbs, only occasionally moderating our exuberance when we went too far, and then making up for it by songs and poems full of fun, and jokes suited to the occasion. Perhaps we did not always quite remember the respect due him, for the ministerial side was, at such times, far less prominent than the playful one. . . .

"We had a little school in the house, and he was constantly in and out of the schoolroom, on most familiar terms with the children, sometimes aiding the discipline, quite as often disturbing it ; and his own room was always a refuge for sad or rebellious scholars.

"Our English governess, a rather timid and narrow churchwoman, had been warned, before entering this Unitarian household, that 'Mr. Sam' was a very radical and dangerous man, and she was anxious accordingly. But as he never talked about his religious views, and she saw only his sweet and genial nature and his childlike ways, she was completely disarmed, and afterwards said that, having known my father and my uncle, she had never been able to say the Athanasian Creed again."

When separated from the different branches of his family, as at Brooklyn and Germantown, Mr. Longfellow forgot the concerns of neither, but kept himself in close connection with them all by correspondence and frequent tokens of affection and interest. His letters to his nieces and nephews were especially charming ; easy and sportive, yet often carrying wise suggestions as to conduct, taste, or grammar, and, when occasion suggested, treating simply, but frankly and impressively, of the deeper themes of the inner life, of duty, of sorrow, of religious faith. He remembered very faithfully birthdays and other anniversaries, and " was always ready with gifts and a verse of fun or sentiment to accompany them. Valentine's Day was never passed without original rhymes and pictures especially adapted to each recipient. For many years, with one or two young assistants, he edited a Christmas paper, made up of clippings collected throughout the year, which were combined and ingeniously adapted, and supplemented, when printed matter failed, by original contributions in prose and poetry." These annual *jeux d'esprit* were read at the principal family gathering, and then circulated among the different homes.

The interest which Mr. Longfellow felt for whatever concerned his young relatives extended to all other youth whom he could reach. In Cambridge he always had a large acquaintance among the students of the college, visiting them in their rooms, bringing them about him in his own, and, with an attraction which seemed magnetic, enlisting their affection and opening avenues of kindly and helpful influence over them. He attended many courses of lectures in the University and it was felt that much of his pleasure in them was derived from the society of the young men whom he thus met. Among the less fortunate youth of the town he was also widely known and trusted. He actively interested himself in the Cambridge "Social Union," an organization for the benefit of young men and boys, and was its vice-president and president, until obliged by increasing age to retire. The "Boys' Aid Club" made him an honorary member, and he went to their meetings, helping them with advice and practical assistance in their plans. "He could pass no boy in the street without some token of kindness, if it was only a touch of the hand as he went by." Once, on a certain field, which was his property, a group of boys had gathered for a game of ball. Seeing him coming they began to run away. But he beckoned to them, and succeeded in inducing them to come to him, when he explained that he was glad to see them in his field, and was willing they should play there as much as they pleased, an announcement which was received with hearty gratitude. At one time, when he lived near a boys' school, he was approached by neighbors for his signature to a petition that the noise they made should be suppressed. "But I *like* their noise," he replied.

XIII

A FEW LETTERS TO A YOUNG FRIEND

WITH one or two youths, Mr. Longfellow established relations of peculiar intimacy. Among these, William Allan Klapp was adopted by him into an affection and watchful interest which were truly parental. It seems desirable to illustrate fully one of Mr. Longfellow's traits which was peculiarly characteristic, and, with that view, the following extracts are appended from his correspondence with this very promising youth (sadly removed by a premature death in 1887), which will help to show his power of reaching the hearts of the young, and how elevating was the influence which he exerted upon them.

LETTERS TO WILLIAM ALLAN KLAPP.

PORTLAND, November —, 1884.

MY BELOVED ALLAN, — I have come down to Portland to our family Thanksgiving ; and being established in the back chamber of the old homestead, I very naturally think of *you*. I believe that to New Englanders Thanksgiving Day is more than to any other people ; its associations running back to days before Christmas was observed in this part of the world.   In my boyhood, even Christmas was not observed, except by the Episcopalians and Roman Catholics (who then were few), and our gifts were always exchanged on New Year's Day.   On Thanksgiving Day, everybody went to "meeting," or church, in the morning, where was always a wonderful and elaborate anthem sung by the choir.   And at dinner were gathered at the old home children and grandchildren, and all the boys and girls were allowed to have as much turkey and as many pieces of mince-pie and pumpkin-pie, and as many nuts and raisins as they could hold. In the evening they played blindman's buff.   As there are no longer any boys and girls in our family, the youngest member being a Junior in college, our gathering is rather soberer and quieter than of yore. . . .

I could not make up my mind to vote for Blaine on the one hand, or for the Democratic party on the other ; so I did not vote at all for presidential electors.   But I think Cleveland will really make a good and independent president. There will be a Republican Senate ; and the Democratic party will be under great inducement to behave well so as to secure a reëlection ; so I hope for the best.

I know you are busy at school, but don't you think you can write me once a month ; say the first Sunday of every month ? I want to know all about you. . . .

The allusions to an "island" in some of the following letters will doubtless be sufficiently clear without particular explanation.

PORTLAND, August 24, 1885.

DEARLY BELOVED, — By this time I hope that all obstacles are cleared away and you are full legal possessors of the island of pines ; I presume that you will not *build* till next spring, as your vacation is so nearly over. But I should think you would like to put up some sort of shelter under which you might camp for a few days. I remember that the boys in the Adirondacks put up, in a few hours, a sort of shanty with poles and a roof of bark, under which they could at least creep for shelter from rain. Is there a rock upon which you could make a fire ? — for you must not set the grass on fire, on any account.

I am not quite sure whether it is the island upon which I landed with you that you have bargained for, or the adjacent one. I feel inclined to buy both ; and authorize you to do so at the same rate as for the first, if you think it desirable. It would secure you from unwelcome neighbors. Are they near enough for a rustic bridge to be made to connect them?

It seems absurd that the house should cost so very much more than the island! There will be time to consider that, and the plan, however, before spring. I shall probably want to help you about it. We will see. Meanwhile it occurs to me that you will have some legal expenses connected with getting possession, and as I wish, at least, to make the island (or islands) my entire gift, you must be sure to let me know the amount.

I am much interested in your appearance in print, and hope soon to see your longer article. I hope you will go on writing. If you can get five dollars a month, it will help towards your building. Why can't you write, with care, " A Summer at Brandt Lake," — just a lively narrative of your doings, — and send it to " Outing." Do it! I shall send you the September number in a day or two. Love to Eugene.

Yours affectionately,   S. L.

CAMBRIDGE, October 6, 1885.

MY DEAR ALLAN, — I congratulate you on your literary successes. I wish that " Outing " would have given you a higher fee, but at the beginning it is a great thing to get your piece and your name into a magazine and before the public. For your next article you had better ask more. You must not expect to see your production printed very soon. They generally have the numbers made up some months ahead.

There seems to be a good deal of delay about getting the title deeds [of the island]; but perhaps by this time it is accomplished. And I hope next summer to be your guest in " Longfellow Lodge." If your room is only ten feet wide outside the bunks, you must have a wide porch outside the door.

I should like to have been with you at Brandt some of these lovely days — warm as summer here. Cambridge is in its autumn glory. College is begun. I know only one Freshman. Oh, Allan, I felt badly to hear that you were not coming to Harvard! But I can see that, living in New York, there may be good reasons for your studying at Columbia.

It seems to me very absurd that the college boys think they cannot play at football for their own enjoyment, without the rivalry of match games. But boys are often unreasonable, are they not?

My book is, at last, in the printer's hands; that is, the first volume. I have still some chapters to write in the second. They do not expect to get it out until after Christmas.

Give my regards to your mother, and my love to Eugene ; and a good deal to yourself.

From your attached   S. L.

CAMBRIDGE, December 31, 1885.

MY DEAR ALLAN, — I am glad you have been enjoying your holidays.   By another week I suppose you will be at your books again.   I rejoice that you are doing well in your studies and hope you have done with "cutting up."   Try to stand as high in character as in your lessons.   It is a great thing for a man to be *high-toned* morally : to have a high sense of what is manly and worthy in motives and aims and principles ; to have a high standard of action that hates everything low.

I notice among the young men here a difference.   Some think only of having a good time in life, or pushing themselves forward in their business or profession, or getting rich, — all their aims ending in themselves.   Others I find interesting themselves in bettering and helping the community in which they live, taking hold, with public spirit, in reform of politics ; or taking part in the Associated Charities or Civil Service Reform associations.   They are not thinking of their own advancement alone, but of doing something for the world, or that part of it in which they live. . . .

CAMBRIDGE, February 20, 1886.

MY VERY DEAR ALLAN, — I am glad that you are not satisfied with a standing which is merely good by comparison with "the other fellows," and that you have a higher standard of your own, namely, what is really good and high. And I hope you will carry this out in other things besides your studies.

I am entirely willing that you should use my Christmas gift for the Society pin. Let it remind you of me, and that I want you to be all that is good and true and noble, — a kind of *talisman*. The motto is good, — is it good Latin? — and is equivalent to "By their fruits ye shall know them." Actions in the long run certainly show what a man is. And yet always what a man or a boy *is*, is even more important than the things he *does*. Do you understand that? . . .

CAMBRIDGE, February 26, 1886.

MY BELOVED ALLAN, — I was rejoiced to hear by your letter that the "red tape" was at last all untied; and trust that the deed is by this time in your possession, and that you are full and legal owner of the green island in Brandt Lake! I enter with all my heart into the pleasure which I imagine you feel in being a "landed proprietor," and the pleasure you and Eugene will have in carrying out your plans of building upon and living upon the island.

There is a little island in Loch Katrine called, from Scott's heroine, "Ellen's Isle." I think I will name yours "Allan's Isle."

I question, however, about the garden which you have laid out upon the plan. I think it would mar the natural surface, the space being so small. Besides it would be too late to plant anything when you go up in summer.

When I think of it, I feel quite impatient for the summer to be here, that I may come and see you in the Lodge, and have a row and a bath.

I took tea on Sunday evening with Mrs. M., sitting at the round table in the dining-room, and wishing you were there.

.   .   .   .

I cannot remember whether I sent you the money for the purchase of the island. You see I am getting old ! Let me know.

CAMBRIDGE, June 8, 1886.

O my dear Allan, what a disappointment ! Of course, we both wish now that we had carried out the plan of buying both islands. However, you must make the best of it now, hard as it is to have so pleasant an anticipation dashed to the ground. I can only hope the lady will get tired of it in a few weeks, or in one summer at least. I do feel quite badly about it, myself, as I had looked forward to my visit to you with so much pleasure.

Meanwhile, be as happy as you can, and don't let yourself be cast down by disappointment, but get some good out of it. You will be sure to have a good time anyway.

CAMBRIDGE, June 30, 1886.

DEAR ALLAN, — I am glad to hear of your success in passing the entrance exams, and hail you as a C-o-l-u-m-b-i-a-n! ("Hail, Columbia" the band will here play). I can't help wishing a little it was Harvard; but that is because I want to have you nearer to me.

To-day has been Commencement day, and a very pleasant one. I heard some of the parts at Sanders Theatre, and attended the Alumni dinner, where were some good speeches, and some dull ones. Two of the speakers spoke strongly against the extravagance and luxury which they thought were increasing among the students. But President Eliot said it was confined to "a very small fraction" of the young men, even of the rich ones. He said it was a mistake to suppose that Harvard was frequented chiefly by the rich; that, besides the large number who had moderate means, actually one in five of the students received pecuniary aid from the college funds.

.   .   .   .

I go to Portland on Saturday for the summer. I wish you were to be in that back chamber again ! . . .

PORTLAND, October 17, 1886.

Still in Portland, and writing at the table in the back chamber, which remembers you, dear Allan.   I can almost see you in this empty chair, half facing me as I write.   What a gift we have in this power by imagination and feeling to live over again scenes long past, and to repeat and prolong the pleasure.   Indeed, we have our pleasures thrice over, — in anticipation, in enjoyment, and in memory.   So "our cup runneth over," as the Psalmist said.   We must remember this in times of disappointment and trouble, and not arraign the good Providence that gives us "richly to enjoy," in giving us the capacity to enjoy and abundant occasions for its exercise.

.   .   .   .

I want to hear more about the island and if anything is decided upon.   Of course, if you can sell the little one for enough to buy the larger, it will be creditable to your business capacity, and a remote tract naturally has a lower market value than one near to human habitations, though it may be worth more to individual tastes and purposes.

.   .   .   .

By the way, I came across your *name* the other day, of all unexpected places, in a poem of Wordsworth's. And, oddly enough, it has reference to a sale of land. I will copy the verse, applying it to the new " Allan's Isle " by changing the first word. When you have become possessor of it, we will say, in view of possible applications to sell again, —

" ' Should the troublesome tempter beset us,' said I.
' Let him come with his purse proudly grasped in his
        hand,
But, Allan, be true to me, — Allan, we 'll die
Before he shall go with an inch of the land ! ' "

This occurs in a poem called " Repentance." In two other books I have just been reading, — or having read to me, — your name is that of the hero. . . .

I go back to Cambridge and Craigie House the 30th of this month. I hope I may welcome you there some day. . . .

Your attached   S. L.

[No date], 1886.

DEARLY BELOVED, — Excuse this half sheet on
which I tell you that, following your wish, I have
directed the publisher to send you a copy of the
"Life" [of Henry W. Longfellow], which accept
with much love from your friend, the editor.

I hope, as you read it, it may inspire you to aim
at a life, like this, of earnest purpose, unflagging
industry, unstained purity, and untiring kindness.

Your attached   S. L.

A *bon voyage*, on Allan's departure for Europe:

[No date.]

Good-by, dear Allan; think of me as always
warmly interested in your welfare.   Keep true to
your best.   God bless you; I say it from my
heart.

Your loving   S. L.

CRAIGIE HOUSE, CAMBRIDGE, January 16, 1887.

DEARLY BELOVED ALLAN, — I am indebted to
you for two letters which I was delighted to get.
I am glad to know that you have such pleasant
quarters.   It is a good deal in a great city to look
upon a garden; even, in winter, to have the open
space, and in the spring it will be pleasant to
watch it growing green.   I shall get out my map
and see if I can find the spot.   I remember Paris

as very gray-skied and drizzly in the winter, the pavements covered with a sticky mud. But the winter was short and the spring delightful, and when the sun shines what a bright and handsome city! . . .

The first winter I spent in Paris — in 1852–53, when Louis Napoleon by a *coup d'état* overthrew the government — I lived in the Rue de la Victoire ; the second winter 1865–66, I lived on the Quai de la Messagerie, near the Place du Châtelet. I never cared for the mass in the Catholic churches, but I used to enjoy going in the afternoon to the Vesper Service, which is almost all music, getting away into some quiet corner to enjoy its devotional feeling.

I have no doubt you are getting on rapidly in speaking French. At first the great thing is to gain fluency, without much regard to accuracy; that is, to talk without minding mistakes, — afterwards taking pains to be correct and grammatical. But from the first take pains to *pronounce* correctly, noticing carefully how the educated French pronounce. One great mistake English and Americans are apt to make is in accenting one syllable of a word strongly and slurring over the others, just as we do in English but as the French do not. Thus the English say *mái*-son, the French *mái-són*, accenting the second syllable as much as the first, though making them both short. So you will hear Americans say Champs Elysées instead of *E-ly̆-sées ;* and *Lúx*embourg instead of *Lúx-ém-boúrg.* Notice, yourself, how the French pronounce these and like words. Plays are good to read, because they give you the language of conversation. I hope you will be able to go to some of the public lectures at the Collége de France. They are free to all, and will train your ear, as well as entertain and instruct you. Remember that the one thing you can do better in Paris than elsewhere is to *learn French ;* therefore do not fail to make good use of this opportunity to learn it *well.* Besides a good pronunciation, there is a peculiar *intonation,* which you can learn only by imitation. You will hear it in every shop, especially where a woman· waits on you. Take notice of it, and try to catch it. There is a sort of turning *up* of the voice at the end of a sentence, whereas in English we turn the voice down. I give you these hints hastily.

But now of this side of the water. . . . I went to Portland for Thanksgiving, and again for Christmas, where we had a merry evening party at my brother Alexander's. I have been writing three articles for a children's magazine, — "The Wide-Awake," — on "Longfellow's Boyhood," "Longfellow with his Children," and " Longfellow with the Children " (not his own).

. . . .

Oh, my dear Allan, I think that little visit of yours here attached me to you more strongly and warmly than ever.   I want you to know how much I prize your affection ; and how warm and deep my friendship for you is.   How I wish it might be of help to you in keeping you up to your best, in keeping you true and high-toned, and above every thing and thought that is low and unworthy.   Set your mark of manhood high. God bless you !   I say it from my heart.

TO THE FATHER OF ALLAN KLAPP, ON RECEIV-ING THE NEWS OF THE YOUNG MAN'S DEATH.

CAMBRIDGE, February 26, 1887.

DEAR MR. KLAPP, — Your telegram is just received.   Oh, my dear sir, what a blow is this! My heart is with you.   But what can I say ? When I think of all that life, that energy, that bright intelligence, that promise of a fine generous manhood !   What hopes you must have centred upon him, and what he would be in the coming years !   And now they are all dashed down !   Not here are they to be fulfilled.   Yet we know not from what he may have been spared. We cannot tell. Perhaps it is well that it is not in our hands to decide. For our very hopes cannot be free from some anxiety for those we love. But I have so often thought, as I looked upon Allan, what a fine manhood was in store for him, with his glow of health, his vigor, his ambition, his active mind.

You know how warmly and strongly attached I had become to him and how much I prized his affection. How hard it is to believe and feel that I shall not look upon his face again ! But I shall always cherish his bright memory, and be glad that I have known him. With no son of my own, I had taken him to my heart.

But it is not perished, — that life, that intelligence, all those qualities that endeared him. Not here, but elsewhere surely they will have their growth and fulfillment. And we shall meet again *there !* For me it will not be very long.

May God console and comfort you ! He is the Heavenly Father. He does not take all sorrow from us, but he gives us strength to bear it, and stands by our side and says, " All shall be well." With strongest and tenderest sympathy,

Your friend,   SAML. LONGFELLOW.

TO ALLAN'S MOTHER.

CAMBRIDGE, June 21, 1887.

MY DEAR MRS. KLAPP,—I thank you very much indeed for the portraits of our dear Allan, and for the paper-knife. You were right in thinking that I should like something which he had *used*. The portraits, especially the larger head, recall him to me distinctly and pleasantly, though I miss the bright coloring. He was very dear to me, as you know. Why should I say *was?* He *is* as much so as ever. He has been often, very often, in my thought. And though, at first, my feeling was a very sad one, that I should never again look into his face, or hear his cheery voice, or witness the unfolding of his manhood out of the bright promise of his boyhood, yet now for me the shadows have passed, and I think of him as he was, so full of life and affection. He seems very near to me, and brings a bright joy to my heart. I hope it is sometimes so with you, though of course to you the sadness of the loss and the disappointment of hopes must be keener and longer enduring. "'T is better to have loved and lost than never to have loved at all," because that which we have once loved is ours forever, by a deep, deep tie of the spirit. The soul holds fast its own. He came into my life, a great happiness to me which I cannot forget or lose. How much more fully can you say this! I do hope, amid all your sorrows, that you have had many happy thoughts of him and can feel his presence. Do not doubt that you are often and deeply in his thoughts and his affectionate heart. Swedenborg says, and I think with truth, that thought and feeling make spiritual *presence*. His nature was indeed (again I ought to say *is*) full of sweetness; and I was much touched with what you wrote me of this, in his illness. His last little visit to me is a great delight to me to remember.

Your friend,

SAMUEL LONGFELLOW.

XIV

THE GERMANTOWN PASTORATE

THE uneventful but happy mode of life which Mr. Longfellow was pursuing in Cambridge was interrupted in the early winter of 1877–78 by an invitation to the pastorate of the Unitarian Society in Germantown, Pennsylvania. His disposition to accept the call was a surprise even to himself. But the union of church and pastor has often been compared to marriage, and its conditions closely resemble those of the personal tie. In this case a congeniality seemed almost immediately to reveal itself between the parties, and they were drawn strongly together. The liberal spirit of the Society; the cordiality and hospitality of its members ; their affectionate union as a congregation ; with the beauty of the town and the pleasant surroundings of the tasteful and homelike church, attracted Mr. Longfellow, as his personal traits and the power and sweetness of his preaching at once charmed the people and led them to the unanimous wish that he should become their pastor. After brief consideration, he responded favorably to their invitation, and was installed their minister on Sunday, January 6, 1878.

The services, by Mr. Longfellow's desire, were brief and informal. An address of welcome and recognition to their new pastor was read, on the part of the people, by the President of the Society, and prayer was offered by the already venerable Dr. Furness. Mr. Longfellow conducted the other exercises of the occasion, and preached the sermon. Its subject was "The Continuity of Life." It was a discourse appropriate to the beginning of a new year and a new ministry. He defined frankly the position he should maintain as the teacher of a pure and simple theism, in absolute mental independence. Recognizing the lofty spiritual and moral qualities of Jesus as a man, and the nobleness of his religious and ethical principles and ideals, he maintained (in consistency with Jesus's own thought) that God, the spiritual Father of men, is the only proper object of worship. He examined the nature of religion, showing that its scope includes the entire area of human relations and activities, and that its truths have their root in the common nature of Deity and Humanity, and in no arbitrary ordinations whatever.

Unequivocal and thorough, the sermon was

listened to with sympathy, even by some to
whom its positions were, as yet, unfamiliar, but
who were commanded by the earnestness and
deeply devout spirit of the preacher and his discourse.

The union thus formed continued, in increasing
happiness and mutual affection, for four and a-
half years. It was marked by few events of
which record can now be made. "I remember
it," writes a gentleman of the Society, "as a
beautiful dream without striking incidents." But
the influence which Mr. Longfellow acquired,
both within and without his congregation, during
this brief period, was singularly deep and wide.
His pastorate was conducted in the same simplicity of method and of manners which had
always been characteristic of him. His preaching, now replete with the wisdom of nearly three-
score years, still dealt preferably with the profound, but simple, themes of the personal life.
Always ethical in emphasis and direction, it was
unvaryingly pervaded by the religious spirit
which experience and reflection made ever surer
and more fervid in him. His hearers hardly
realized (it was said) how profoundly and search-
ingly he had touched and moved them, until they
had left the presence of the preacher. It was by
the power of the truth, discerned and felt, unec-

statically but most practically, and accepted with unqualified sincerity and absolute loyalty into his own life. "He carried into deeds all that he preached." The divine quality of human nature ; men's direct relations to God ; his constant presence in their lives ; his perfect accessibility, were, to Samuel Longfellow, realities so vivid that, averse as he was to formal utterance of religious feelings, they moulded and shone through all his conversation, and seemed, even to his countenance and the intonations of his voice, to give their indescribable grace and purity.

In the homes of his new congregation Mr. Longfellow speedily established himself as a familiar presence. Observing no regular system of visiting, he seemed, by a happy tact, to be habitually among them, and especially to be with them when peculiar joys or sorrows intervened in the tenor of their experience. One who had known a great affliction said, " He did not make me formal visits, nor remain long with me when he called, nor speak much of my trial and its supports ; but almost daily I received some reminder of his sympathy, and it seemed as if, through his being with me, the truths I needed to support me had made their way to my heart. . . .

"It was on Sunday morning when Mr. Longfellow came, while the church bells were still ringing, and prayed with us. And such a prayer! I seem to hear it now, and to feel the calm that entered into my soul. What he was to me and my children in the weary days that followed, it is not in the power of language to convey. Not one single day for weeks did he omit coming to see us, and he never failed to leave a blessing behind. My anxieties for my family were very great; but, after a visit from Mr. Longfellow, I felt *sure* the way would be opened by which I should be able to provide for them, although I cannot recall that he ever made any suggestion as to what I could do. But one felt the power of his own trust and faith. . . .

"By the way, he made a beautiful distinction between trust and faith. Trust says, 'O Lord, Thy will be done.' Faith says, 'I come, O Lord, to do Thy will.' . . .

"At one time I had been disposed to look rather on the hardships than on the mercies of my lot. He spoke no word of reproof, but, soon after, sent me a card with these lines : —

'Though but one berry on the spray should ripen;
Though but one spray upon the bough grow green;
Though but one bough above the tree-top brighten,
God's power and goodness in that one are seen.'

. . . "He carried into deeds all that he preached. In every charitable work which he proposed to his congregation it was ' let *us* ' do so and so."

Into the joys as well as the trials of his people ; their lighter as well as their graver concerns ; the pleasures of the young ; family anniversaries, Mr. Longfellow entered so naturally and sympathetically, according to the spirit of each occasion, that he was everywhere the most welcome of all guests to old and young. His traits of character revealed themselves peculiarly in the friendly notes, always short, which, under various circumstances, he was led to write to his parishioners. The deepest truths were conveyed in a few suggestive words, made convincing and persuasive by their perfect spontaneousness. His sense of humor was very quick, and his faculty of sportive verse enhanced the merriment of many an occasion of gladness, as his tender and serious lines helped sorrowful hearts to rise above their grief.

In his personal mode of life, during these years, Mr. Longfellow found a fresh interest and pleasure, with something of amusement. Most of the time he had his own house, assuming the novel responsibilities of bachelor housekeeping, and much enjoying the opportunity of exercising hospitality.

TO MRS. G. L. S.

GERMANTOWN, ——, 1878.

DEAR FRIEND, — Your delicate vase is on the desk before me, with a more delicate rosebud, lifting up its beautiful head to praise God by showing forth his beauty, and serve Him by gladdening human hearts. What a psalm it sings!

I have just come in from my morning walk in this soft, radiant day. A tender mist half veiled the bare gray woodlands, and the cypress-like evergreen cedars threw blue shadows on the snow. . . .

Will you believe that I am really at housekeeping? A very pleasant sunny house, furnished, even with a cook, was offered me at a very reasonable price. After four days' experience, I can say that housekeeping is very nice! I try to catch somebody to dine with me, and usually take tea out in the parish.

I felt at home in Germantown from the first, and I have been very happy since I came back. I must go to my sermon. With true regards,

S. L.

TO MRS. G. L. S.

GERMANTOWN, April 1, 1878.

DEAR FRIEND, — To-day there are violets in the little vase, from my garden-bed. For the spring is here. And on my table a bunch of Mayflowers brought from the woods by one of my boys. We miss this year the joyful contrast of winter and spring, having had only spring. For myself, I think a week of real winter is enough.

And you, I hope, are out among your trees in the sunshine, busy perhaps with your garden-shears in teaching your vines and shrubs to keep the limits of beauty, saying to them, "Thus far and no farther," and so helping God — who needs so much human help — to make the world right. And there in the sunshine and the new life, a soft dirge sounds in your heart, — a threnody.

> "I touch this flower of silken leaves
> Which once *his* childhood knew ;
> Its soft leaves wound me with a grief
> Whose balsam never grew.
>
> .   .   .   .
>
> I see my trees repair their boughs,
>
> .   .   .   .
>
> Returned this day, the south wind searches
> And finds young pines and budding birches,
> But finds not the budding man!"

But spring whispers its word of hope and restoration, and all things point onward.

My life flows on quite busily and very pleasantly. I fall back into the pastoral life as naturally as if I had never left it. Did I write you that I was keeping house? I like it, though it is a little solitary. But I fancy its solitude is preferable to the society of a boarding-house.

TO MRS. G. L. S.

GERMANTOWN, January 18, 1879.

MY DEAR FRIEND, — The little vase to-day holds a half-open white camellia and a spray of dark purple heliotrope. Are there not some days and some experiences, all fair and unshadowed, which yet bear in them none of the spiritual fragrance that comes from the heart of darkly shadowed ones? That thought or fancy came to me as I looked at the flowers. I wonder what meaning you would have read in them?

I have delayed for too long, not to thank you for your kind remembrance and the Emerson, — that I did at once, — but *to tell you* that I thanked you. But you were sure of it, — we are always sure of our friends so far as that. But if we do not hear we are not sure that our gift ever reached them.

We have had the bare earth till now, which I

don't like to lose from my eyes; but now the snow lies over all.   The white snow is to me like the white camellia, beautiful but heartless.   Still, it gives the boys snowballing and coasting and sleigh-rides; and to poor men the chance to earn a little with their shovels.   Did you ever see the story of the tramp, who, begging in August, was asked, "Why don't you work?"   Said he, "There is nothing doing now in *my* business."   "And what is your business?"   "Shoveling snow."

But if the snow is cold, the golden sunsets are not; how radiant and transparent!   And this morning I saw a golden sunrise — from my pillow.

Among the guests in Mr. Longfellow's home, it was natural that the young should be especially welcome.   Living near the large Germantown Academy (the picturesque old building of which peculiarly interested him), he became familiarly acquainted with the pupils, whose sports he loved to watch, and who learned to confide frankly in him.   He went frequently among them, and they came often in groups or singly to his house.   For their freer access, he had a gateway opened in his fence.   It was, perhaps, one of these boys who afterwards said, "I used to be very much ashamed to have anybody caress me in the presence of others; but when Mr. Longfellow did so, I felt proud and happy." But with boys in all parts of the town Mr. Longfellow established an acquaintance. Many were familiar with him who did not know his name. "That kind gentleman" was a title which, as in another town, was applied to him by one of these.

A gentleman, searching for Mr. Longfellow's house, asked a street boy to direct him to it. The answer told its own story. "What! Don't you know *him*? Why every one knows where *he* lives!"

It must be confessed that to his kind words and ways he added certain innocent, tangible attractions. "A friend of mine," writes a lady, "saw him on the street one winter's morning, with each arm around a shabbily dressed boy, while he was encouraging a third to search the pockets of his overcoat. She could not resist awaiting the result, and the urchin discovered *candy!*" Another writes, "Once, in a provision store, I met Mr. Longfellow looking at apples. He was picking out a barrel, that the Academy boys might help themselves when they came to his house, and he asked me if I did not think 'that boys liked *red* apples best.'"

He loved to gather children about his bachelor

table, and make them feel at home in his house. It was quite usual to find several little people engaged with him in talk, or amusing themselves with his books and pictures. "One day when I stopped to see him on some church-work, I found him with a boy (quite a little one) on each side of him and a huge book of animals open before them. Knowing that he had some fine illustrated fairy stories, I reminded him that the children would enjoy those. But Mr. Longfellow replied, 'No, not these little *Friends;* we like the animals and birds best.' Later, he told me that he always put his imaginative books away when those boys visited him, fearing that he might show them something which their Quaker parents might not like."

One very little fellow became at last impressed with a deficiency in this household of one. Dining with him, the child suddenly observed, "But, Mr. Longfellow, where is your *wife?*" "I have none," was the reply. "You have n't *got* any?" (incredulously). "No, I have n't any." "Did n't you *ever* have one?" "No." "*Why* did n't you?" "Perhaps I never found the right one." "Did you *hunt* after her?" "At this point," said Mr. Longfellow, much amused at the incident, "I thought it time to turn the conversation."

But fond as he was of all children, some of the little girls had a feeling that his preference was for the boys. One of them taxed him with this, and commissioned a friend to demand why it should be so. He seemed to admit the partiality when, after a moment, he replied, "Tell her it is, perhaps, because I never *was* a little girl."

Mr. Longfellow's spirit of charity led him into a similar wide acquaintance among the humble families of the town. In his quiet but observant way, he discovered many cases of suffering and want, and brought them relief, either through public agencies or from his own means, which were always disproportionately taxed for objects of kindness. The poor knew and loved him as the children did.

But his sympathy went out especially to those burthened by the distresses of the mind and heart. To hear of persons in trouble, or doubt, or sorrow was, with him, to seek out some way of reaching them with comfort, or guidance, or encouragement, often while he remained un-known.

" Mr. Longfellow's æsthetic instincts," writes a friend, "and his love for historical associations led him to take a great interest in the *old* things of Germantown ; his liking for the quaint people in their odd little shops, with their conservative

ways, offered a marked contrast to his progressive
tendencies in thought.   During his last visit to
us he said, referring to the changes taking place
in town, the pulling down of old houses, 'I don't
like *changes;* I hope they will leave *some* of the
old places, for we need links with the past generations; there are few enough in America at
the best.'

"The only time I ever heard him quote from
his brother's writings, in private, was in speaking
of my grandfather's house and the alterations
which had been made in it during fifty years
past, when he repeated from 'The Golden Mile-
stone,' —

> " ' Happy he whom neither wealth nor fashion
>   Nor the march of the encroaching city
>   Drives an exile
>   From the hearth of his ancestral homestead.' "

Another of his parishioners writes as follows : —

"I hardly know how to convey my impressions
of Mr. Longfellow's influence in Germantown,
for his whole personality was so essentially spiritual that it eludes one's effort to portray it in
words.   When, later, he died, I felt that the
transition from this world to the world of spirit
would be to him a very natural change, — a much
shorter step than it could be in most lives, — for

there seemed to be in his nature so little that tied him to earthly things.

"He was not an active worker in the days when we knew him ; largely because of his delicate health, but also from temperament. He thought, truly, that the weight of one's personal influence lent to any cause was always one's best assistance to it. What he *was*, was always much more important than what he did. He strongly disliked *argument*, and had a quiet way of letting a subject drop and introducing a new topic if there seemed to be danger of increasing warmth in a conversation. He had no desire to convince others that they were in the wrong, except by standing himself quietly and firmly on the other side.

"In this way there sometimes seemed in him a lack of warmth, which made him more especially the preacher to the older and maturer minds of his congregation, rather than to the glowing enthusiasts of our younger circle.

"Yet many of his quiet bits of philosophy sank deeply into our young hearts, and were a real balm for us in that time of stress and strain which comes to those who, while feeling that they must struggle for something higher, are not quite sure of their aim. I remember one sermon, in particular, on 'Secondary Motives.'

It was, in the main, a plea for conventionality, that bugbear of youth, and he said that to do a thing because it was polite was almost always to do it because it was *kind;* that in most ways the laws of society had grown to be a code of kindness and consideration for others, and in general they were safer to follow than one's own crude sense of ideal propriety.

" His attitude on the subject of Temperance at one time disturbed me a little ; but I found an answer to my questionings in a sermon he preached upon ' Evil,' — the misuse of good, the good gone wrong; that only in perfect liberty can there be perfect obedience to law ; and my mind settled itself upon this subject for all time.

" I remember a phrase which he used in a marriage-service, which was thoroughly characteristic and showed his fondness for putting his own interpretation into others' words.   In pronouncing the benediction he said, ' *If* God has joined . . . let no man put asunder.'

" He had the deepest appreciation of home and home life ; and we all of us wished that his own experience might have included that love which alone gives ideal beauty and blessing to home life.   In a letter to me he wrote the following childlike sentiment : ' I am glad you are so happy in your new life, and I see no reason why your happiness should not continue and increase. I remember once being told by a lady, whom I knew when a young boy, that love is often stronger after marriage than before.'

" This gives a glimpse, I think, into his entirely theoretical relations to this subject."

In this connection the following letter may be inserted, although written by Mr. Longfellow in 1857.

" Your marriage day is very near, and before my return you will have begun your new life and departed for your new home. As I cannot be with you in person at this time, I must let my pen do its office, at least so far as to assure you that an occasion so full of interest to you cannot fail to be of interest to me, and that I enter with friendly sympathy into the new hopes that open before you.

" Doubtless those hopes, however warmly they glow in your heart, still float somewhat vaguely in your thoughts, and your ideal of a true married life lies high and beautiful yet undefined in the heavens of your soul. And as the months of reality go by, the hope and the ideal may fade somewhat. Do not be disappointed if they do ; do not expect an immediate realization of them. Yet, I beseech you, do not give up the hope, nor let the ideal go ; recognize the present limitations ; yet fulfill, as much as you can, your best thought of what the relation should be and should accomplish. At first, doubtless, your affection will make all the new duties easy ; but the time must come when you will need patience and self-sacrifice and a strong sense of duty. These will deepen the love and spiritualize it and keep it strong and true enough to meet every emergency.

"It is much that any man has given his happiness into your keeping. But that is not all. For it is more to feel that another's spiritual life is, in a great measure, in your charge. It has been said of the true wife that, ' with a heart at once pious and large, she forever *improves* the man she has wedded.'

"To call out all this highest nature, to sympathize with and encourage every noblest purpose and aspiration, — this is indeed a high and beautiful service for one soul to do for another. And this is what husband and wife can do, as perhaps none others can.

"That you will find this accomplished for you and your husband, I sincerely hope. That your union will be a spiritual union, a sympathy and communion of your inmost natures, I earnestly trust. Then it will be indeed the beginning of new life to you. For true spiritual love is the image and presence of God, and when it dwells in a soul God dwells there. May his blessing accompany all your way!"

While still living in Germantown, a genuine sorrow befell Mr. Longfellow in the death of his friend Samuel Johnson. The two had been profoundly intimate for forty years. Their thoughts had flowed in parallel channels; their principles and aims were completely harmonized. Their habits and modes of life were similar. In temperament, they were sufficiently contrasted to make friendship delightful and intercourse mutually helpful. The advanced position which both held in religion and philosophy, and the strong bent of their minds to individualism in thought and action, largely isolated them from other thinkers and workers in their chosen field, and made the confidence they gave each other, and their community of views, the more precious to each. Their personal association was close and constant; their correspondence frequent, and as affectionate and interesting on the part of Mr. Johnson as we have found it to be on the part of Mr. Longfellow.

Such a friendship could not be suspended by the parting of death without a deep sense of bereavement to the survivor; nor could it end on earth without its memorial. During the year following Mr. Johnson's death, Mr. Longfellow (as has already been mentioned) gathered up some of his lectures, essays, and sermons into a volume, prefixing a memorial sketch through which the love he bore his friend, and the admiration he felt for his character, talents, and scholarship, and for his services to morals and to literature, are brightly conspicuous.

It was a still nearer bereavement, following closely upon the other, which led to the termination of Mr. Longfellow's beautiful ministry in Germantown. In March, 1882, died his beloved brother Henry. From the death-bedside and funeral of the poet he returned to his people full of tender feeling, but oppressed by no gloom of sorrow. On the following Sunday he preached to them an uplifting sermon, into which the spiritual experiences of the time were gathered, full of faith and thankfulness. But the duty at once occurred, which no other could so fittingly discharge, of preparing a memoir of his brother. He very soon announced to his congregation that, on this account, he must withdraw from them, and although the parting was an occasion of sorrowful regret to all, the necessity for it was fully recognized.

XV

RESIGNING his pulpit, in 1882, Mr. Longfellow returned to Cambridge, and took up his abode again in the familiar Craigie House. How much he had come to be at home in Germantown, he was made aware as he revived old associations. "I was surprised to find," he wrote, "that I felt quite strange in coming back to my old quarters." His affections were never weaned from his Germantown people, and so long as he lived he maintained friendly relations with them, interchanging frequent letters and other tokens of regard with some who had been peculiarly intimate with him.

TO MRS. H. M. S.

CAMBRIDGE, May 27, 1883.

. . . I have been doing a good deal of gardening the last fortnight, and trust the seeds I have sown will repay me for my tired back. But it is quite an act of *faith* (almost as much as preaching sermons, the sowing of spiritual seeds) when one remembers that the seed is not always good, and that sometimes there is too much rain, and sometimes too hot a sun ; and that if the birds of the air do not carry them off, sometimes Satan in the form of small Irish boys carries off the plants bodily ; as has happened to some of my handsome pansies. But I am glad that they like flowers. It might be good for them if I should set out some of the plants called " Honesty." . . .

TO MRS. C. B.

CAMBRIDGE, September 23, 1883.

I have been grieved to hear, within a few days, that your health, which I had hoped and believed quite restored, is not yet established. I know your courage and patience will not fail you in this longer trial, nor your trust in the Father's infinite goodness and the nearness of his presence to help us bear every burden. The burden He does not always take away ; but He lightens it, oh, how much ! by the tender trust in his power to make all things work for good. I hope you may be already regaining your strength, but most of all I pray that you may every hour be "strengthened with all might in the inner man," renewed "day by day." How many things are explained by this our double life, the outward and the inward, and how the experiences of life teach us that it is the inward that is the real and the significant and the lasting. I am sure that the more we are accustomed to look at things in their inward bearing and aspect and consequences, the more truly we see them as God sees and means them. And in that way we find many things in his providence made clearer which else would seem dark and strange. But how beautiful, also, it is to trust, where we cannot see, and to believe, where we cannot explain! . . .

TO MRS. H. M. S.

CAMBRIDGE, November 19, 1884.

It is snowing outside, and I am here alone, in the study, with a fire and a pen.

What a contrast to the Indian summer days I left in Germantown! Perhaps they have ended even there; but I don't believe it is snowing.

My visit was a delightful one, and it was a charming way to end up the season. The country, so lovely in its sober late autumn colors of olive and russet and deep red; the friendly greetings and hospitalities; the lunches, the dinners, the teas; the pictures at the Academy; the happiness of the wedding; the hours in the church, — all these things live in memory. How good God is to us, so to fashion our natures that we can enjoy not only the actual having of things, but the memory of them ; and often we must add the anticipation, making a threefold enjoyment. . . .

Mr. Chadwick and the church in Brooklyn to which I once ministered wish me to come and take part in the twentieth anniversary of my successor's installation. What a long ministry, for these days ! Should you think he would have anything left to say ? But some things have to be said over more than once. . . .

TO MRS. G. L. S.

[During a visit to Germantown.]

GERMANTOWN, April 21, 1886.

. . . I am enjoying to the full the exquisite pleasure of the unfolding green ; the trees not yet " clothed upon," but just veiled ; a bed of white violets under my window, Forsythia and the Japanese quince ; by the roadside the blue violet. Oh, the enchantment, the magic, the sweet miracle of nature's ways ! the stones made bread and the water turned to wine for the hunger and thirst of our souls ! This beautiful world we live in and the Supreme Beauty it hides and reveals ! These costly pictures given freely to every passerby ! Oh, the depth of the riches of the goodness of God !

The gift comes to each of us as if made especially for him, and yet to each of us, if we think of it, enhanced by its being meant and made for *all*, and for each only as one of the all.

And now, as I look out, the white violets have taken wings and are flying about above the beds like white butterflies.

That is the Easter symbol, and shall be my Easter greeting.

TO MRS. H. M. S.

CAMBRIDGE, May 20, 1886.

. . . It seems to me most reasonable and right to believe that the thoughts and affections of those who have passed through the veil are still with us, as ours are with them. All that is "gone" is the visible and tangible form in which the thoughts and affections were enshrined. And that is much, for it is endeared to us as expressing the inward and invisible person whom we really love ; but the spirit is not gone, for I cannot believe that the dropping-off of the body, which is only its garment, can change *that*.

XVI

THE BIOGRAPHY

SETTLED in familiar Cambridge, Mr. Longfellow applied himself diligently to the biography of his brother, which occupied him quite fully for nearly four years. He felt that of one whose works had made him so widely known and loved, there should exist an exhaustive account; while he wished and trusted that, from it, memoirs, briefer and adapted to wider circulation, might be composed. He even urged upon Mr. James Russell Lowell, who had lately completed such a biography of Hawthorne, to write a one-volume memoir of his neighbor and friend and brother-poet. Mr. Longfellow's own work was one of devoted love and reverence for the man, as well as admiration for the poet, and he spared no pains to give it accuracy and completeness. But he rejoices when the long task is ended!

TO MRS. H. M. S.

CAMBRIDGE, December 31, 1885.

I am like a schoolboy who begins to see the vacation approaching. In a month from now my work will be done, and the burden rolled off from my shoulders.

I want the publishers to issue it on February 27, the poet's birthday. There is so little of incident and adventure in the life of a literary man that only those who are already interested in his writings will find interest in his biography. There will be plenty of faults in my work, some of which I shall see for the first time when the book is printed and bound, but I shall not tell anybody what they are. . . .

TO A SISTER.

February 17, 1886.

And so my long work is finished ! I can hardly tell how it has lasted so long. But a large part of it makes no appearance in the book, — the reading, sifting, choosing, deciding, rejecting; yet, on the whole, I am well satisfied. Do you know that letters do not read as well in print as in manuscript ? . . .

TO MRS. H. M. S.

CAMBRIDGE, 1886.

. . . I think you will find a singular *unity* running through the book in several ways. Those who knew my brother personally will recognize the same qualities of character in the man that were in the boy, only that the quick temper was completely controlled. Then his early purpose of distinction in literature, beginning at seventeen, in college, and fulfilling itself at seventy, never lost sight of in the interval. One might even note the interest in the Indians shown in his first poor printed poem, coming out in college in an exhibition dialogue, then in mid-life culminating in " Hiawatha." You will observe also the gentle *humor* that runs through his letters and diaries, something of which you noticed in " Outre-Mer."

We have had a wonderfully pleasant March. What an exhilaration of feeling comes with the first spring days ; and what pleasant associations from away back in childhood !

Do you remember a pleasant-faced youth whom I brought one evening to our church parlor, a young artist? Son of a Methodist clergyman, he has become, mostly by his own reflection and study, a Unitarian, so he writes me. I believe more would do so, if they did a little more *thinking*. . . .

Mr. Longfellow's life, while engaged upon the memoir, was of the quietude and sunny cheerfulness which were characteristic of him. Its one especial incident was the occurrence of his seventieth birthday, June 18, 1889. The observance of the anniversary by his friends, and their kind forethought to make it happy, touched him tenderly, as appears in some of the letters which follow.

TO MRS. G. L. S.

INTERVALE, July 22, 1888.

"And the mountains shall bring peace," says the Hebrew prophet. Can I send you some of the restfulness of this interval amongst the hills? Here all is strength and beauty, not sublimity or terror. The ranges of hills which encircle us for four fifths of our horizon do not imprison, but only guard us. The loftier peaks and slopes are just far enough away to take on every lovely change of blue, in turn. The nearer wooded hills show all tints of green, light or dark as sunshine or cloud-shadow lies upon them, and at evening sink into a deep velvet hue that has no name. Wordsworth says of his hero that, returning at night, he "saw all the hills grow larger in the dark." But it is not so here; to my eye they look distinctly smaller. One hesitates to differ from so close an observer as Wordsworth. I think his line may be true of hills that are very near to the observer.

.   .   .   .

Did I ever tell you that when, as a little child, I said my prayers, I always thought that "thine be the glory " meant the " morning-glory " ?   So it is my sacred flower.

TO MRS. G. L. S.

CRAIGIE HOUSE, January —, 1890.

Your red and white azaleas stand shining upon the table before me.   What vigorous flowers they are, and so generous!

With their green leaves and ferns they make the Italian colors.   Do you remember the story of the Italian prima.donna who, singing in Milan, under the old Austrian oppression, when every Italian manifestation was forbidden — I have really forgotten *what* she did (so I hope you *do* remember), but in some way, by means of flowers, she indicated her love of Italy and hatred of Austria. — Now it comes to me!   When the patriots in the audience threw her bouquets of red, white, and green, she placed them in her bosom ; the authorities then forbade her to pick them up.   The next night they threw on the stage bouquets of the Austrian colors, and she quietly walked over them, thus treading them under her feet. . . .

TO MRS. G. L. S.

[No date.]

I thought of you in the still solitude of Willoughby Lake, and wished that you might have entered into its quiet. Yet where could you go that you would not feel the something that *should be there* to satisfy the hunger of your heart, and *is not?*

When years and years have knit the outward ties and twined them so closely with the inward that they grow as indistinguishable almost as color and fragrance in the flower, how can that all be changed, "in an instant," and the tendrils of our every feeling be torn off that which they clung to and grew into, without unspeakable desolation and bewildered sense of loss? How long will it take to exchange, at every point, this outward for the inward it signifies, the twined spiritual and material for the spiritual alone? How long? How often that question must arise in your heart! Yet it will come; you cannot tell when. Not with observation, not all at once, — the peace that passeth understanding. Already you have experience of it in some calm sweet hours of spiritual presence. And then will more and more be vouchsafed to you, and the tossed waves of your heart spread out into still waters.

By such lake-sides of the Spirit I hope you have often been sitting, and seen the heavens reflected in that uplifting calm, as at Willoughby we used to see the sunset glories in the sky and water between the sentinel cliffs.

I hope, at least, that to your ear may come the bird-song, which, because it is a voice, touches our hearts more deeply than even the flowers can do, in their silence.

But if you are shut from these too, may the Spirit visit you, not through symbols, but by that immediate vision and presence, — that secret whisper to the soul which fills it with holy peace, as it leads to the green pastures and still waters, as you lay your troubled heart to rest in the ever-lasting arms ! So prays for you

Your friend,　　　　　　　　S. L.

TO A SISTER.

CAMBRIDGE, June 20, 1889.

Thanks for the beautiful little pencil. It will be in constant use, and constantly remind me of the giver. I have a particular liking for *small* things. I do not know whether it is a sign of advancing age. I find that even my handwriting grows smaller. It is not yet as small as Mr. G.'s, which was nearly invisible in his last years. Henry's remained large and firm to the last.

You will want to know about the birthday.
The affair opened by the arrival of the first guest
on Monday afternoon.   Mrs. Fields came up
from Manchester to attend our niece's afternoon
reception to the working-women from some of
the Boston stores.   About thirty of them wan-
dered through the rooms and walked in the garden and sat on the piazza.   I read to them the
account of the Craigie House from " The Life,"
and she read some of the poems. . . . Mrs. Fields
brought me a box of lovely delicate and fragrant
sweet-brier roses.   The next morning she presented me with a fine etched portrait of James
Martineau, a strong and earnest face.   At breakfast came a great bunch of carnations from one
of my boy friends ; then a box of fine red roses
from Mrs. Spellman ; then came C. with her
smallest boy bringing a bouquet.   Flowers poured
in during the day.   Dear Mrs. Nichols sent a
pretty basket of roses set in a glass of water so
that they did not have to be removed ; Wentworth Higginson a large basket of "seventy
roses ; " M. a bouquet with white roses from the
old Portland bush ; C. a box of fine florist's roses,
— and so on.   There were notes from Edward
Hale and Sam Eliot, both of whom had engage-
ments elsewhere.   About five o'clock came William and Harriet P., bringing a large book and a

small one, the latter a tiny scrap-book, in which, at the age of eleven, I had copied some verses, as we used to do.

Presently A. came to me and said, "It can be kept secret no longer ; come into the front parlor and see your surprise."   I went, and found Mr. Kneisel, Mr. Loeffler, and Mr. Foote, with piano, violin, and 'cello, who said they would play me some trios of Beethoven.   Others came in, and the music was delicate and charming.   Ices and strawberries were served, and all was very pleasant and cordial.

TO MRS. G. L. S.

CAMBRIDGE, June 19, 1889.

Seventy thanks, or, seventy times seven, for your beautiful and thoughtful gifts on my birthday !

I did very much hope that you would yourself be able to come.   I would have found a quiet corner for you in the front parlor, where a few of us sat awhile and listened to such music as would have charmed and rested you. . . .

Some fifty of my Cambridge friends came with kind greetings and flowers, and warmed the cool day with their friendliness.   It was very pleasant, and I was not at all tired.   When I woke up this morning at six o'clock, I felt decidedly *younger ;* but now I have got back into seventy again.

But it is much to be thankful for, — I am not forgetful of it, — to have lived seventy happy, peaceful, and not useless years. And what a time to have been living in !

The wreath was exquisite, in the most delicate tints of rose and white and pale yellow, — as lovely as a Beethoven trio.

Ever your obliged   S. L.

John Holmes, some years my senior, sent me some very nice stanzas, as good as his brother would have written.

XVII

LAST DAYS

THE gentle, gracious life of Samuel Longfellow was now near its peaceful close.

In the late autumn of 1891, a sorrow fell upon the household of one of his brothers, and he went to Portland to be with the family. "A more lovely, calming influence in a home was never known." There was no apprehension at the time that he would be the next to leave the earthly circle of his friends and relatives. Yet his vigor was noticeably impaired, and during the visit, while he never alluded to his condition, he sometimes seemed languid, and even depressed.

The next July he went again to his native city, and spent several weeks in the ancient house where he was born. He was now distinctly unwell, the disease from which he had been for so many years a sufferer evidently making rapid progress. But in August he was able to join his brother's family at the seashore, on Cape Elizabeth, a few miles from Portland. Here ensued a sudden and violent attack, which the physicians at once pronounced the beginning of the end. After a little time he rallied, and for a few weeks it was even hoped that he was not to be called away. His old friend Edward Everett Hale came to see him, and their meeting was most merry, full of boyish recollections and mutual reminders of early days, of woodland rambles and boating-excursions in Portland harbor, when neither of them knew much of the sailor's craft. His relatives were constantly about him, but their fond wish, and his own, that he might be removed again to one of their homes, and especially to that which had been his birthplace, could not be gratified. He expressed no disappointment, and spoke only once of the change which was plainly approaching. He had been slightly wandering in mind, then became quiet, and it was thought that he was sleeping. Presently, quite in his natural voice, he spoke to a young relative at his bedside, asking if she recalled the lines of Whittier's " Hampton Beach," beginning

> " The soul may know
> No fearful change, nor sudden wonder.
> Nor sink the weight of mystery under.
> But with the upward rise, and with the vastness grow."

These he repeated almost entire, adding from the following stanza,

> "Familiar as our childhood's stream,
> Or pleasant memory of a dream."

In the early morning of October 3d, just as the sunlight was beginning to stream into the room, in perfect peace, he died.

A few days later, in the ancient homestead where he was born, brief exercises of devotion and commemoration were conducted amidst the family to whom he had been so dear. A public service followed, in the old First Parish Church, where he had been taught to worship as a child. Thence his remains were carried to the family tomb in the Western Cemetery, a picturesque, overgrown retreat, very quiet and rural, and a fitting resting place for what was mortal of Samuel Longfellow.

AFTER this book was ready for the press, information was received that on Sunday, March 25, 1894, a bronze tablet to the memory of Mr. Longfellow was unveiled in their church, by the Second Unitarian Society of Brooklyn. It bears the following inscription : —

SAMUEL LONGFELLOW

MINISTER

OF THIS SOCIETY FROM APRIL 1853 TO JUNE 1860.
A MAN OF GENTLE NATURE, LIBERAL CULTURE, LOVING
HEART · A FAITHFUL PREACHER AND PASTOR · EARNEST
IN REFORM · THE FRIEND OF LITTLE CHILDREN.
A POET OF RELIGION, HE GAVE US MANY PERFECT
SONGS OF HOPE AND CHEER.
BORN JUNE 13. 1819 ✠ DIED OCTOBER 3, 1892.
"TO BE SPIRITUALLY MINDED IS LIFE AND PEACE."

www.ingramcontent.com/pod-product-compliance
Lightning Source LLC
Chambersburg PA
CBHW031031120726
47905CB00007B/2144